MONT/

Selections from the Essays

TRANSLATED AND EDITED BY

Donald M. Frame

COLUMBIA UNIVERSITY

Crofts Classics

GENERAL EDITORS
Samuel H. Beer, *Harvard University*
O. B. Hardison, Jr., *Georgetown University*

HARLAN DAVIDSON, INC.
Arlington Heights, Illinois 60004

Copyright © 1943 by Walter J. Black, Inc.
Copyright renewed 1971 by Donald M. Frame
Copyright © 1948, 1957, 1958 by the Board of Trustees
of the Leland Stanford Junior University
Reprinted 1973 by arrangement with Stanford University Press
All Rights Reserved

This book, or parts thereof, must not be used or reproduced in
any manner without written permission. For information,
address the publisher, Harlan Davidson, Inc., 3110 North
Arlington Heights Road, Arlington Heights, Illinois 60004-1592.

Library of Congress Catalog Card Number: 72-96557
ISBN 0-88295-105-X

Manufactured in the United States of America
90 89 33 34 35 MG

Contents

Important Dates in Montaigne's Life

1533   Michel Eyquem de Montaigne is born at the Château de Montaigne (not far from Bordeaux) on February 28. He is taught Latin from the cradle, and no French until he is six.

1539–1546   Studies at the Collège de Guienne in Bordeaux.

1554   Counselor at the Cour des Aides in Périgueux.

1557   The Cour des Aides incorporated into the Parlement (a sort of supreme court) of Bordeaux. Montaigne a counselor there.

1558–1563   Friendship with Etienne de La Boétie, ended by his death.

1559–1560   Death of Henry II of France (1559). Francis II succeeds, dies (1560), succeeded in turn by Charles IX under regency of his mother Catherine de' Medici.

1562–1598   Religious wars in France between Catholics and Protestants, almost uninterrupted and increasingly political.

1564   Birth of Galileo and of Shakespeare, who was to be a reader of Montaigne in John Florio's English translation (1603).

1565   Montaigne marries Françoise de la Chassaigne.

1568   Death of Montaigne's father Pierre. Michel now lord of Montaigne.

1569   Translation from Latin of Raymond Sebond's *Theologia naturalis*.

1571   Montaigne retires and soon starts to write.

1572   St. Bartholomew's Day Massacre of Protestants by Catholics.

1574   Death of Charles IX. Accession of Henry III.

1576–1578   Montaigne has a medal struck bearing a pair of scales in balance. He is made Gentleman of the Chamber by King Henry of Navarre. He begins to suffer from the kidney stone.

1580–1583   First edition of the *Essays*, Books I and II (1580). Hoping to cure his illness, Montaigne sets out for Rome via the mineral baths of Switzerland, Germany, and Italy. He keeps a diary, discovered and published in 1774. Elected Mayor of Bordeaux while still in Rome (1581), he accepts when ordered to by Henry III. He is re-elected in 1583.

1585   End of Montaigne's mayoralty. Plague in and around Bordeaux.

1586–1588   Montaigne returns to the *Essays*, adds to Books I and II, writes Book III, publishes fifth edition in three books.

1589   Henry III assassinated. Henry of Navarre succeeds as Henry IV.

1590   Henry IV invites Montaigne to come to court. Montaigne too ill to accept.

1592   Montaigne dies of quinsy on September 13.

Introduction

"I am myself the matter of my book," Montaigne wrote in 1580 in his preface. He knew by then what he had not fully known when he started to write his *Essays* eight years before: that any book is bound to be a book about its author. This necessity became his conscious purpose. But because his goal was not yet fully clear, he called his book *essais*, that is to say *tests* or *trials:* trials, as he tells us later, of his judgment and his natural faculties.

Before he finished, Montaigne's concept of his book had greatly expanded. He saw that you cannot write about yourself without writing directly or indirectly about all mankind. His subject became a twofold study of himself and of man, with the purpose of finding the way for himself to live and principles of living for others.

He also came to see that his book had a life of its own. Written over a period of twenty years, added to but little corrected, it showed him the change as well as the continuity in himself and reminded him that to show us life he must show us change: "I do not portray being: I portray passing." That this led to apparent inconsistency did not matter: "I do indeed contradict myself now and then; but truth . . . I never contradict." Knowing that change was inevitable, he was unafraid of it and willing to accept it whenever it seemed good. Thus his book helped him actually to fashion himself: "I have no more made my book than my book has made me—a book consubstantial with its author, concerned with my own self, an integral part of my life."

This is no exaggeration. A well-to-do Gascon nobleman, taught to speak Latin before he spoke French, Montaigne retired at thirty-eight, after twenty years as counselor-at-law, from the weary slavery of the courts, as he put it, to freedom and calm in the bosom of the learned muses. He had lost his dear friend Etienne de La Boétie and the father he loved; he was dutifully married; he had published a successful translation. In his study in the tower of Montaigne he loved to read. Out of the notes he took grew the rather bookish early essays; out of these grew the two books of personal and original essays that he published after nine years of retirement.

Then for recreation and health he set out on a roundabout trip to Rome. To his surprise, in his absence he was elected Mayor of Bordeaux and instructed to accept by King Henry III. He promised nothing, but did well enough to be re-elected after two years. The bloody religious and political civil wars between Catholics and Protestants were in full fury. Disillusioned but loyal, he admired his Protestant friend Henry of Navarre, but supported his Catholic king, Henry III.

After his mayoralty and a period of flight with his family from the plague, he returned to his *Essays,* published the fifth edition in three books, and continued until he died to add to his great work.

The *Essays* are so varied that Montaigne has been many things to his many readers. It was long assumed that the core of his thought was the systematic skepticism of the long and central "Apology for Raymond Sebond." Recent students have stressed the culmination of his thought, the confident affirmation of Book III. Montaigne was both skeptical and positive. His question "What do I know?" was not just a passing doubt. He was always very conscious of one of the bases of skepticism, the fact that no two things, no two men's opinions, no two opinions of one man at different times, are ever alike. "Resemblance," he says in his last essay, "does not make things as much alike as difference makes them unlike." But he was also and increasingly aware of likeness. If men were not different, he points out, we could not tell them apart; if they were not similar, we could not tell them from the animals. The function of experience, the ultimate method of truth for Montaigne, is to do in its humble way what it can do more surely than its prouder colleague reason: to sift the elements of similarity from the chaos of fact into some pattern that men can live by.

The wisdom that Montaigne seeks from his study of man is the knowledge of how to live. Not that he believes there is just one way for all men to live; on the contrary, each man must follow his own nature. But we must learn our nature before we can follow it; we must know ourselves before we can become ourselves.

We cannot go wrong if we follow nature. The vices that Montaigne hates—cruelty, lying, hypocrisy—he does not consider truly natural. Conversely, the only goodness for him is the easy goodness that practice has made a second nature. He respects moral codes more exacting than his own, but experience has taught him how often by trying for too much we achieve too little. "Instead of changing into angels, they change into beasts." Montaigne knows that there are sincere idealists among truly religious men. But he also knows how few men have true religion, and he writes mainly for those who have not.

Our greatest trouble, he concludes, is that we forget what we are here for and spend ourselves on trifles. Our job is not to rule, to hoard, to build; it is to live appropriately. We assume that this is easy; it is not. It is a life study, an exacting art. It is also the greatest and most important art of all, the art of happiness, the very purpose of our life. "It is an absolute perfection and virtually divine to know how to enjoy our being lawfully."

The superscript letters [ABC] in the text serve to distinguish the three certain strata in which the *Essays* were composed:

[A] designates material published before 1588 (generally in 1580 unless otherwise noted);
[B] designates material published in 1588;

^C designates material published after 1588.

This is my own translation. It is based largely on Pierre Villey's second edition of the *Essais*, Paris, Alcan, 1930-1931, 3 volumes. The translations of Montaigne's Latin quotations are nearly all my own.

BIBLIOGRAPHY

Auerbach, Erich, "L'Humaine Condition," in *Mimesis: The Representation of Reality in Western Literature,* translated by Willard R. Trask, pp. 285-311. Princeton, Princeton University Press, 1953.

Emerson, Ralph Waldo, "Montaigne; or, the Skeptic," in *Representative Men.*

Frame, Donald M., *Montaigne: A Biography,* New York, Harcourt, Brace and World, 1965.

Friedrich, Hugo, *Montaigne,* translated by Rovini, Paris, Gallimard, 1968. In French.

Friedrich, Hugo, *Montaigne,* Bern, Francke, 1949. Revised edition, 1967. In German.

Gide, André, "Presenting Montaigne," translated by Dorothy Bussy, in *The Living Thoughts of Montaigne,* pp. 1-27. New York and Toronto, Longmans, Green, 1939.

Lüthy, Herbert, "Montaigne, or the Art of Being Truthful," *Encounter,* November 1953, pp. 33-44; also in Quentin Anderson and Joseph A. Mazzeo, editors, *The Proper Study,* New York, St. Martin's Press, 1962, pp. 318-336.

Montaigne, *Oeuvres complètes,* edited by Albert Thibaudet and Maurice Rat, Paris, Gallimard, 1962. Pléiade edition.

Montaigne, *The Complete Works,* translated by Donald M. Frame, Stanford, Stanford University Press, 1957.

Sainte-Beuve, C.-A., "Montaigne," in *Causeries du lundi,* translated by E. J. Trechmann, vol. VI, pp. 61-77. London: Routledge, and New York: Dutton, 1909, 8 vols.

Woolf, Virginia, "Montaigne," in *The Common Reader,* pp. 87-100. New York, Harcourt Brace, 1925.

BOOK I

To the Reader

ᴬThis book was written in good faith, reader. It warns you from the outset that in it I have set myself no goal but a domestic and private one. I have had no thought of serving either you or my own glory. My powers are inadequate for such a purpose. I have dedicated it to the private convenience of my relatives and friends, so that when they have lost me (as soon they must), they may recover here some features of my habits and temperament, and by this means keep the knowledge they have had of me more complete 10 and alive.

If I had written to seek the world's favor, I should have bedecked myself better, and should present myself in a studied posture. I want to be seen here in my simple, natural, ordinary fashion, without straining or artifice; for it is myself that I portray. My defects will here be read to the life, and also my natural form, as far as respect for the public has allowed. Had I been placed among those nations which are said to live still in the sweet freedom of nature's 20 first laws, I assure you I should very gladly have portrayed myself here entire and wholly naked.

Thus, reader, I am myself the matter of my book; you would be unreasonable to spend your leisure on so frivolous and vain a subject.

So farewell. Montaigne, this first day of March, ᴵ fifteen hundred and eighty.

Of Idleness[1]

[A]Just as we see that fallow land, if rich and fertile, teems with a hundred thousand kinds of wild and useless weeds, and that to set it to work we must subject it and sow it with certain seeds for our service; and as we see that women, all alone, produce mere shapeless masses and lumps of flesh, but that to create a good and natural offspring they must be made fertile with a different kind of seed; so it is with minds. Unless you keep them busy with some definite subject
10 that will bridle and control them, they throw themselves in disorder hither and yon in the vague field of imagination.

> [B]Thus, in a brazen urn, the water's light
> Trembling reflects the sun's and moon's bright rays,
> And, darting here and there in aimless flight,
> Rises aloft, and on the ceiling plays.
>
> VIRGIL

[A]And there is no mad or idle fancy that they do not bring forth in this agitation:

20 > Like a sick man's dreams,
> They form vain visions.
>
> HORACE

The soul that has no fixed goal loses itself; for as they say, to be everywhere is to be nowhere:

> [B]He who dwells everywhere, Maximus, nowhere dwells.
>
> MARTIAL

[A]Lately when I retired to my home, determined so far as possible to bother about nothing except spending the little life I have left in rest and seclusion, it seemed to me I could do my mind no greater favor
30 than to let it entertain itself in full idleness and stay

1. Chapter 8.

4

and settle in itself, which I hoped it might do more easily now, having become weightier and riper with time. But I find—

> Ever idle hours breed wandering thoughts
>
> LUCAN

—that, on the contrary, like a runaway horse, it gives itself a hundred times more trouble than it took for others, and gives birth to so many chimeras and fantastic monsters, one after another, without order or purpose, that in order to contemplate their ineptitude and strangeness at my pleasure, I have begun to put them in writing, hoping in time to make my mind ashamed of itself.

Of the Education of Children[1]

To Madame Diane de Foix, Comtesse de Gurson

^AI have never seen a father who failed to claim his son, however mangy or hunchbacked he was. Not that he does not perceive his defect, unless he is utterly intoxicated by his affection; but the fact remains that the boy is his. And so I myself see better than anyone else that these are nothing but reveries of a man who has tasted only the outer crust of sciences in his childhood, and has retained only a vague general

10 picture of them: a little of everything and nothing thoroughly, French style. For to sum up, I know that there is such a thing as medicine, jurisprudence, four parts in mathematics, and roughly what they aim at. ^C And perhaps I also know the service that the sciences in general aim to contribute to our life. ^ABut as for plunging in deeper, or gnawing my nails over the study of Aristotle, ^Cmonarch of modern learning, ^Aor stubbornly pursuing some part of knowledge, I have never done it; ^Cnor is there an art of which I could sketch

20 even the outlines. There is not a child halfway through school who cannot claim to be more learned than I, who have not even the equipment to examine him on his first lesson, at least according to that lesson. And if they force me to, I am constrained, rather ineptly, to draw from it some matter of universal scope, on which I test the boy's natural judgment: a lesson as strange to them as theirs is to me.

I have not had regular dealings with any solid book, except Plutarch and Seneca, from whom I draw like

30 the Danaïds, incessantly filling up and pouring out.

1. Chapter 26.

6

Some of this sticks to this paper; to myself, little or nothing.

[A]History is more my quarry, or poetry, which I love with particular affection. For as Cleanthes said, just as sound, when pent up in the narrow channel of a trumpet, comes out sharper and stronger, so it seems to me that a thought, when compressed into the numbered feet of poetry, springs forth much more violently and strikes me a much stiffer jolt. As for the natural faculties that are in me, of which this book is the essay, I feel them bending under the load. My conceptions and my judgment move only by groping, staggering, stumbling, and blundering; and when I have gone ahead as far as I can, still I am not at all satisfied: I can still see country beyond, but with a dim and clouded vision, so that I cannot clearly distinguish it. And when I undertake to speak indiscriminately of everything that comes to my fancy without using any but my own natural resources, if I happen, as I often do, to come across in the good authors those same subjects I have attempted to treat—as in Plutarch I have just this very moment come across his discourse on the power of imagination—seeing myself so weak and puny, so heavy and sluggish, in comparison with those men, I hold myself in pity and disdain.

Still I am pleased at this, that my opinions have the honor of often coinciding with theirs, [C]and that at least I go the same way, though far behind them, saying "How true!" [A]Also that I have this, which not everyone has, that I know the vast difference between them and me. And nonetheless I let my thoughts run on, weak and lowly as they are, as I have produced them, without plastering and sewing up the flaws that this comparison has revealed to me. [C]One needs very strong loins to undertake to march abreast of those men. [A]The undiscerning writers of our century who amid their nonexistent works scatter whole passages of the ancient authors to do themselves honor, do just the opposite. For this infinite difference in brilliance gives so pale, tarnished, and ugly an aspect to the part that is their own that they lose in this way much more than they gain.

^CThere were two contrasting fancies. The philosopher Chrysippus mixed into his books, not merely passages, but entire works of other authors, and in one the *Medea* of Euripides; and Apollodorus said that if you cut out of them all the foreign matter, the paper he used would be left blank. Epicurus, on
80 the contrary, in three hundred volumes that he left, put in not a single borrowed quotation.

^AI happened the other day to come upon such a passage. I had dragged along languidly after French words so bloodless, fleshless, and empty of matter and sense that they really were nothing but French words. At the end of a long and tedious road I came upon a bit that was sublime, rich, and lofty as the clouds. If I had found the slope gentle and the climb a bit slower, it would have been excusable; but it
90 was a precipice so straight and steep that after the first six words I realized that I was flying off into another world. From there I saw the bog I had come out of, so low and deep that I never again had the stomach to go back down into it. If I stuffed one of my chapters with these rich spoils, it would show up too clearly the stupidity of the others.

^CTo criticize my own faults in others seems to me no more inconsistent than to criticize, as I often do, others' faults in myself. We must denounce them
100 everywhere and leave them no place of refuge. Still, I well know how audaciously I always attempt to match the level of my pilferings, to keep pace with them, not without a rash hope that I may deceive the eyes of the judges who try to discover them. But this is as much by virtue of my use of them as by virtue of my inventiveness or my power. And then, I do not wrestle with those old champions wholesale and body against body; I do so by snatches, by little light attacks. I don't go at them stubbornly;
110 I only feel them out; and I don't go nearly as much as I think about going. If I were a match for them

I would be a good man, for I take them on only at their stiffest points.

As for doing what I have discovered others doing, covering themselves with other men's armor until they don't show even their fingertips, and carrying out their plan, as is easy for the learned in common subjects, with ancient inventions pieced out here and there—for those who want to hide their borrowings and appropriate them, this is first of all injustice and 120 cowardice, that, having nothing of their own worth bringing out, they try to present themselves under false colors; and second, it is stupid of them to content themselves with gaining deceitfully the ignorant approbation of the common herd, while discrediting themselves in the eyes of men of understanding, whose praise alone has any weight, and who turn up their nose at our borrowed incrustations. For my part, there is nothing I want less to do. I do not speak the minds of others except to speak my own mind better. This 130 does not apply to the compilations that are published as compilations; and I have seen some very ingenious ones in my time; among others, one under the name of Capilupus, besides the ancients. The minds of these authors are such that they stand out in this sort of writing as well as in other kinds, as does Lipsius in the learned and laborious web of his *Politics.*

^AHowever that may be, I mean to say, and whatever these absurdities may be, I have had no intention of concealing them, any more than I would a bald 140 and graying portrait of myself, in which the painter had drawn not a perfect face, but mine. For likewise these are my humors and opinions; I offer them as what I believe, not what is to be believed. I aim here only at revealing myself, who will perhaps be different tomorrow, if I learn something new which changes me. I have no authority to be believed, nor do I want it, feeling myself too ill-instructed to instruct others.

Well, someone who had seen the preceding article[2] was telling me at my home the other day that I should 150

2. The chapter "Of Pedantry" (I:25).

have enlarged a bit on the subject of the education
of children. Now, Madame, if I had some competence
in this matter, I could not use it better than to make
a present of it to the little man who threatens soon
to come out so bravely from within you (you are
too noble-spirited to begin otherwise than with a male).
For having had so great a part in bringing about your
marriage, I have a certain rightful interest in the
greatness and prosperity of whatever comes out of
160 it; besides that, the ancient claim that you have on
my servitude is enough to oblige me to wish honor,
good, and advantage to all that concerns you. But
in truth I understand nothing about it except this,
that the greatest and most important difficulty in
human knowledge seems to lie in the branch of
knowledge which deals with the upbringing and education of children.
        ^CJust as in agriculture the operations that come
before the planting, as well as the planting itself, are
170 certain and easy; but as soon as the plant comes to
life, there are various methods and great difficulties
in raising it; so it is with men: little industry is needed
to plant them, but it is quite a different burden we
assume from the moment of their birth, a burden full
of care and fear—that of training them and bringing
them up.
        ^AThe manifestation of their inclinations is so slight
and so obscure at that early age, the promises so
uncertain and misleading, that it is hard to base any
180 solid judgment on them. ^BLook at Cimon, look at
Themistocles and a thousand others, how they belied
themselves. The young of bears and dogs show their
natural inclination, but men, plunging headlong into
certain habits, opinions, and laws, easily change or
disguise themselves.
        ^AStill it is difficult to force natural propensities.
Whence it happens that, because we have failed to
choose their road well, we often spend a lot of time
and effort for nothing, training children for things
190 in which they cannot get a foothold. At all events,

in this difficulty, my advice is to guide them always to the best and most profitable things, and to pay little heed to those trivial conjectures and prognostications which we make from the actions of their childhood. ^CEven Plato, in his *Republic*, seems to me to give them too much authority.

^AMadame, learning is a great ornament and a wonderfully serviceable tool, notably for people raised to such a degree of fortune as you are. In truth, it does not receive its proper use in mean and lowborn 200 hands. It is much prouder to lend its resources to conducting a war, governing a people, or gaining the friendship of a prince or a foreign nation, than to constructing a dialectical argument, pleading an appeal, or prescribing a mass of pills. Thus, Madame, because I think you will not forget this element in the education of your children, you who have tasted its sweetness and who are of a literary race (for we still have the writings of those ancient counts of Foix from whom his lordship the count your husband and 210 yourself are descended; and François, Monsieur de Candale, your uncle, every day brings forth others, which will extend for many centuries the knowledge of this quality in your family), I want to tell you a single fancy of mine on this subject, which is contrary to common usage; it is all that I can contribute to your service in this matter.

The task of the tutor that you will give your son, upon whose choice depends the whole success of his education, has many other important parts, but I do 220 not touch upon them, since I cannot offer anything worth while concerning them; and in this matter on which I venture to give him advice, he will take it only as far as it seems good to him. For a child of noble family who seeks learning not for gain (for such an abject goal is unworthy of the graces and favor of the Muses, and besides it looks to others and depends on them), or so much for external advantages as for his own, and to enrich and furnish himself inwardly, since I would rather make of him an able 230 man than a learned man, I would also urge that care be taken to choose a guide with a well-made rather than a well-filled head; that both these qualities should be required of him, but more particularly character and understanding than learning; and that he should go about his job in a novel way.

Our tutors never stop bawling into our ears, as though they were pouring water into a funnel; and our task is only to repeat what has been told us.
240 I should like the tutor to correct this practice, and right from the start, according to the capacity of the mind he has in hand, to begin putting it through its paces, making it taste things, choose them, and discern them by itself; sometimes clearing the way for him, sometimes letting him clear his own way. I don't want him to think and talk alone, I want him to listen to his pupil speaking in his turn. ^CSocrates, and later Arcesilaus, first had their disciples speak, and then they spoke to them. *The authority of those who teach*
250 *is often an obstacle to those who want to learn* [Cicero].

It is good that he should have his pupil trot before him, to judge the child's pace and how much he must stoop to match his strength. For lack of this proportion we spoil everything; and to be able to hit it right and to go along in it evenly is one of the hardest tasks that I know; it is the achievement of a lofty and very strong soul to know how to come down to a childish gait and guide it. I walk more firmly
260 and surely uphill than down.

If, as is our custom, the teachers undertake to regulate many minds of such different capacities and forms with the same lesson and a similar measure of guidance, it is no wonder if in a whole race of children they find barely two or three who reap any proper fruit from their teaching.

^ALet him be asked for an account not merely of the words of his lesson, but of its sense and substance, and let him judge the profit he has made by the
270 testimony not of his memory, but of his life. Let

him be made to show what he has just learned in a hundred aspects, and apply it to as many different subjects, to see if he has yet properly grasped it and made it his own, ^Cplanning his progress according to the pedagogical method of Plato. ^AIt is a sign of rawness and indigestion to disgorge food just as we swallowed it. The stomach has not done its work if it has not changed the condition and form of what has been given it to cook.

^BOur mind moves only on faith, being bound and 280 constrained to the whim of others' fancies, a slave and a captive under the authority of their teaching. We have been so well accustomed to leading strings that we have no free motion left; our vigor and liberty are extinct. ^C*They never become their own guardians* [Seneca]. ^BI had a private talk with a man at Pisa, a good man, but such an Aristotelian that the most sweeping of his dogmas is that the touchstone and measure of all solid speculations and of all truth is conformity with the teaching of Aristotle; that outside 290 of this there is nothing but chimeras and inanity; that Aristotle saw everything and said everything. This proposition, having been interpreted a little too broadly and unfairly, put him once, and kept him long, in great danger of the Inquisition at Rome.

^ALet the tutor make his charge pass everything through a sieve and lodge nothing in his head on mere authority and trust: let not Aristotle's principles be principles to him any more than those of the Stoics or Epicureans. Let this variety of ideas be set before 300 him; he will choose if he can; if not, he will remain in doubt. ^COnly the fools are certain and assured.

^AFor doubting pleases me no less than knowing.

DANTE

For if he embraces Xenophon's and Plato's opinions by his own reasoning, they will no longer be theirs, they will be his. ^CHe who follows another follows nothing. He finds nothing; indeed he seeks nothing. *We are not under a king; let each one claim his own*

310 *freedom* [Seneca]. Let him know that he knows, at least. ^He must imbibe their ways of thinking, not learn their precepts. And let him boldly forget, if he wants, where he got them, but let him know how to make them his own. Truth and reason are common to everyone, and no more belong to the man who first spoke them than to the man who says them later. ^CIt is no more according to Plato than according to me, since he and I understand and see it in the same way. ^AThe bees plunder the flowers here and there,

320 but afterward they make of them honey, which is all theirs; it is no longer thyme or marjoram. Even so with the pieces borrowed from others; he will transform and blend them to make a work that is all his own, to wit, his judgment. His education, work, and study aim only at forming this.

^CLet him hide all the help he has had, and show only what he has made of it. The pillagers, the borrowers, parade their buildings, their purchases, not what they get from others. You do not see the gratuities

330 of a member of a Parlement, you see the alliances he has gained and honors for his children. No one makes public his receipts; everyone makes public his acquisitions.

The gain from our study is to have become better and wiser by it.

^AIt is the understanding, Epicharmus used to say, that sees and hears; it is the understanding that makes profit of everything, that arranges everything, that acts, dominates, and reigns; all other things are blind,

340 deaf, and soulless. Truly we make it servile and cowardly, by leaving it no freedom to do anything by itself. Who ever asked his pupil what he thinks ^Bof rhetoric or grammar, or ^A of such-and-such a saying of Cicero? They slap them into our memory with all their feathers on, like oracles in which the letters and syllables are the substance of the matter. ^CTo know by heart is not to know; it is to retain what we have given our memory to keep. What we know rightly we dispose of, without looking at the model,

without turning our eyes toward our book. Sad compe- 350
tence, a purely bookish competence! I intend it to
serve as decoration, not as foundation, according to
the opinion of Plato, who says that steadfastness,
faith, and sincerity are the real philosophy, and the
other sciences which aim at other things are only
powder and rouge.

ᴬI wish Paluel or Pompey,[3] those fine dancers of
my time, could teach us capers just by performing
them before us and without moving us from our seats,
as those people want to train our understanding without 360
setting it in motion; ᶜor that we could be taught to
handle a horse, or a pike, or a lute, or our voice,
without practicing at it, as those people want to teach
us to judge well and to speak well, without having
us practice either speaking or judging.

ᴬNow, for this apprenticeship, everything that
comes to our eyes is book enough; a page's prank,
a servant's blunder, a remark at table, are so many
new materials.

For this reason, mixing with men is wonderfully 370
useful, and visiting foreign countries, not merely to
bring back, in the manner of our French noblemen,
knowledge of the measurements of the Santa Rotonda,
or of the richness of Signora Livia's[4] drawers, or,
like some others, how much longer or wider Nero's
face is in some old ruin there than on some similar
medallion; but to bring back knowledge of the characters and ways of those nations, and to rub and polish
our brains by contact with those of others. I should
like the tutor to start taking him abroad at a tender 380
age, and first, to kill two birds with one stone, in
those neighboring nations where the language is farthest from our own and where the tongue cannot be
bent to it unless you train it early.

Likewise it is an opinion accepted by all, that it

3. Ludovico Palvalli and Pompeo Diobono, two famous Milanese
dancing masters at the French court.
4. Probably a Roman dancer of Montaigne's time.

is not right to bring up a child in the lap of his parents.
This natural love makes them too tender and lax,
even the wisest of them. They are capable neither
of chastising his faults nor of seeing him brought up
390 roughly, as he should be, and hazardously. They could
not endure his returning sweating and dusty from his
exercise, ^Cdrinking hot, drinking cold, ^Aor see him
on a skittish horse, or up against a tough fencer, foil
in hand, or with his first harquebus. For there is no
help for it: if you want to make a man of him,
unquestionably you must not spare him in his youth,
and must often clash with the rules of medicine:

> ^BLet him live beneath the open sky
> And dangerously.

400   HORACE

^CIt is not enough to toughen his soul; we must
also toughen his muscles. The soul is too hard pressed
unless it is seconded, and has too great a task doing
two jobs alone. I know how much mine labors in
company with a body so tender and so sensitive, which
leans so hard upon it. And I often perceive in my
reading that in their writings my masters give weight,
as examples of great spirit and stoutheartedness, to
acts that are likely to owe more to thickness of skin
410 and toughness of bones. I have seen men, women,
and children naturally so constituted that a beating
is less to them than a flick of the finger to me; who
move neither tongue nor eyebrow at the blows they
receive. When athletes imitate philosophers in endurance, their strength is that of sinews rather than
of heart....
^AHe will be taught not to enter into discussion or
argument except when he sees a champion worth
wrestling with, and even then not to use all the tricks
420 that can help him, but only those that can help him
most. Let him be made fastidious in choosing and
sorting his arguments, and fond of pertinence, and
consequently of brevity. Let him be taught above-all
to surrender and throw down his arms before truth

as soon as he perceives it, whether it be found in the hands of his opponents, or in himself through reconsideration. For he will not be set in a professor's chair to deliver a prepared lecture. He is pledged to no cause, except by the fact that he approves of it. Nor will he take up the trade in which men sell for 430 ready cash the liberty to repent and acknowledge their mistakes. ᶜ *Nor is he forced by any necessity to defend everything that has been prescribed and commanded* [Cicero].

If his tutor is of my disposition, he will form his will to be a very loyal, very affectionate, and very courageous servant of his prince; but he will cool in him any desire to attach himself to that prince otherwise than by sense of public duty. Besides several other disadvantages which impair our freedom by these 440 private obligations, the judgment of a man who is hired and bought is either less whole and less free, or tainted with imprudence and ingratitude. A courtier can have neither the right nor the will to speak and think otherwise than favorably of a master who among so many thousands of other subjects has chosen him to train and raise up with his own hand. This favor and advantage corrupt his freedom, not without some reason, and dazzle him. Therefore we generally find the language of those people different from any other 450 language in a state, and little to be trusted in such matters.

ᴬLet his conscience and his virtue shine forth in his speech, ᶜand be guided only by reason. ᴬLet him be made to understand that to confess the flaw he discovers in his own argument, though it be still unnoticed except by himself, is an act of judgment and sincerity, which are the principal qualities he seeks; ᶜthat obstinacy and contention are vulgar qualities, most often seen in the meanest souls; that 460 to change his mind and correct himself, to give up a bad position at the height of his ardor, are rare, strong, and philosophical qualities.

ᴬHe will be warned, when he is in company, to

have his eyes everywhere; for I find that the chief places are commonly seized by the least capable men, and that greatness of fortune is rarely found in combination with ability. While people at the upper end of a table were talking about the beauty of a tapestry

470 or the flavor of the malmsey, I have seen many fine sallies wasted at the other end. He will sound the capacity of each man: a cowherd, a mason, a passer-by; he must put everything to use, and borrow from each man according to his wares, for everything is useful in a household; even the stupidity and weakness of others will be an education to him. By taking stock of the graces and manners of others, he will create in himself desire of the good ones and contempt for the bad.

480 Put into his head an honest curiosity to inquire into all things; whatever is unusual around him he will see: a building, a fountain, a man, the field of an ancient battle, the place where Caesar or Charlemagne passed:

^BWhich land is parched with heat, which numb with frost,
What wind drives sails to the Italian coast.

PROPERTIUS

^AHe will inquire into the conduct, the resources, and the alliances of this prince and that. These are things

490 very pleasant to learn and very useful to know.

In this association with men I mean to include, and foremost, those who live only in the memory of books. He will associate, by means of histories, with those great souls of the best ages. It is a vain study, if you will; but also, if you will, it is a study of inestimable value, ^Cand the only study, as Plato tells us, in which the Lacedaemonians had kept a stake for themselves. ^AWhat profit will he not gain in this field by reading the *Lives* of our Plutarch?

500 But let my guide remember the object of his task, and let him not impress on his pupil so much ^Cthe date of the destruction of Carthage as the characters of Hannibal and Scipio, nor so much ^Awhere Marcellus

died as why his death there showed him unworthy
of his duty. Let him be taught not so much the histories
as how to judge them. ^CThat, in my opinion, is of
all matters the one to which we apply our minds in
the most varying degree. I have read in Livy a hundred
things that another man has not read in him. Plutarch
has read in him a hundred besides the ones I could 510
read, and perhaps besides what the author had put
in. For some it is a purely grammatical study; for
others, the skeleton of philosophy, in which the most
abstruse parts of our nature are penetrated.

^AThere are in Plutarch many extensive discussions,
well worth knowing, for in my judgment he is the
master workman in that field; but there are a thousand
that he has only just touched on; he merely points
out with his finger where we are to go, if we like,
and sometimes is content to make only a stab at the 520
heart of a subject. We must snatch these bits out
of there and display them properly. ^BJust as that
remark of his, that the inhabitants of Asia served
one single man because they could not pronounce
one single syllable, which is "No," may have given
the matter and the impulsion to La Boétie for his
Voluntary Servitude. ^AJust to see him pick out a trivial
action in a man's life, or a word which seems unimpor-
tant: that is a treatise in itself. It is a pity that men
of understanding are so fond of brevity; doubtless 530
their reputation gains by it, but we lose by it. Plutarch
would rather we praised him for his judgment than
for his knowledge; he would rather leave us wanting
more of him than satiated. He knew that even of
good things one may say too much, and that Alexan-
dridas justly reproached the man who was talking
sensibly but too long to the ephors: "O stranger, you
say what you should, but otherwise than you should."
^CThose who have a thin body fill it out with padding;
those who have slim substance swell it out with words. 540

^AWonderful brilliance may be gained for human
judgment by getting to know men. We are all huddled
and concentrated in ourselves, and our vision is

reduced to the length of our nose. Socrates was asked where he was from. He replied not "Athens," but "The world." He, whose imagination was fuller and more extensive, embraced the universe as his city, and distributed his knowledge, his company, and his affections to all mankind, unlike us who look only
550 at what is underfoot. When the vines freeze in my village, my priest infers that the wrath of God is upon the human race, and judges that the cannibals already have the pip. Seeing our civil wars, who does not cry out that this mechanism is being turned topsy-turvy and that the judgment day has us by the throat, without reflecting that many worse things have happened, and that ten thousand parts of the world, to our one, are meanwhile having a gay time? [B]Myself, considering their licentiousness and impunity, I am amazed to
560 see our wars so gentle and mild. [A]When the hail comes down on a man's head, it seems to him that the whole hemisphere is in tempest and storm. And a Savoyard said that if that fool of a French king had known how to play his cards right, he would have had it in him to become chief steward to the duke of Savoy. His imagination conceived no higher dignity than that of his master. [C]We are all unconsciously in this error, an error of great consequence and harm. [A]But whoever considers as in a painting the great picture of our
570 mother Nature in her full majesty; whoever reads such universal and constant variety in her face; whoever finds himself there, and not merely himself, but a whole kingdom, as a dot made with a very fine brush; that man alone estimates things according to their true proportions.

This great world, which some multiply further as being only a species under one genus, is the mirror in which we must look at ourselves to recognize ourselves from the proper angle. In short, I want it
580 to be the book of my student. So many humors, sects, judgments, opinions, laws, and customs teach us to judge sanely of our own, and teach our judgment to recognize its own imperfection and natural

weakness, which is no small lesson. So many state disturbances and changes of public fortune teach us not to make a great miracle out of our own. So many names, so many victories and conquests, buried in oblivion, make it ridiculous to hope to perpetuate our name by the capture of ten mounted archers and some chicken coop known only by its fall. The pride and 590 arrogance of so many foreign displays of pomp, the puffed-up majesty of so many courts and dignities, strengthens our sight and makes it steady enough to sustain the brilliance of our own without blinking. So many millions of men buried before us encourage us not to be afraid of joining such good company in the other world. And likewise for other things....

ᴬTo the examples may properly be fitted all the most profitable lessons of philosophy, by which human actions must be measured as their rule. He will be 600 told:

ᴮWhat you may justly wish; the use and ends
Of hard-earned coin; our debt to country and to friends;
What heaven has ordered us to be, and where our stand,
Amid humanity, is fixed by high command;
What we now are, what destiny for us is planned;

PERSIUS

ᴬwhat it is to know and not to know, and what must be the aim of study; what are valor, temperance, and justice; what the difference is between ambition and 610 avarice, servitude and submission, license and liberty; by what signs we may recognize true and solid contentment; how much we should fear death, pain, and shame;

ᴮWhat hardships to avoid, what to endure, and how;

VIRGIL

ᴬwhat springs move us, and the cause of such different impulses in us. For it seems to me that the first lessons in which we should steep his mind must be those that regulate his behavior and his sense, that will teach 620 him to know himself and to die well and live well.

^CAmong the liberal arts, let us begin with the art that liberates us....

It is a strange fact that things should be in such a pass in our century that philosophy, even with people of understanding, should be an empty and fantastic name, a thing of no use and no value, ^Cboth in common opinion and in fact. ^AI think those quibblings which have taken possession of all the approaches to her
630 are the cause of this. It is very wrong to portray her as inaccessible to children, with a surly, frowning, and terrifying face. Who has masked her with this false face, pale and hideous? There is nothing more gay, more lusty, more sprightly, and I might almost say more frolicsome. She preaches nothing but merrymaking and a good time. A sad and dejected look shows that she does not dwell there. Demetrius the grammarian, finding a group of philosophers seated together in the temple of Delphi, said to them: "Either
640 I am mistaken, or, judging by your peaceful and gay countenances, you are not engaged in any deep discussion." To which one of them, Heracleon the Megarian, replied: "It is for those who are inquiring whether the verb βάλλω has a double λ, or seeking the derivation of the comparatives χεῖρον and βέλτιον and the superlatives χεῖριστον and βέλτιστον, to knit their brows when discussing their science. But as for the teachings of philosophy, they are wont to delight and rejoice those who discuss them, not to make them sullen
650 and sad."

> ^BYou'll find the hidden torments of the mind
> Shown in the body, and the joys you'll find;
> The face puts on a cloak of either kind.

JUVENAL

^AThe soul in which philosophy dwells should by its health make even the body healthy. It should make its tranquillity and gladness shine out from within; should form in its own mold the outward demeanor, and consequently arm it with graceful pride, an active
660 and joyous bearing, and a contented and good-natured

countenance. ^CThe surest sign of wisdom is constant cheerfulness; her state is like that of things above the moon, ever serene. ^AIt is *Baroco* and *Baralipton*[5] that make their disciples dirt-caked and smoky, and not she; they know her only by hearsay. Why, she makes it her business to calm the tempests of the soul and to teach hungers and fevers to laugh, not by some imaginary epicycles, but by natural and palpable reasons. ^CShe has virtue as her goal, which is not, as the schoolmen say, set on the top of a 670 steep, rugged, inaccessible mountain. Those who have approached virtue maintain, on the contrary, that she is established in a beautiful plain, fertile and flowering, from where, to be sure, she sees all things beneath her; but you can get there, if you know the way, by shady, grassy, sweetly flowering roads, pleasantly, by an easy smooth slope, like that of the celestial vaults. It is because they have not associated with this virtue—this supreme, beautiful, triumphant, loving virtue, as delightful as she is courageous, a pro- 680 fessed and implacable enemy of sourness, displeasure, fear, and constraint, having nature for her guide, fortune and pleasure for companions—that there are men who in their weakness have made up this stupid, sad, quarrelsome, sullen, threatening, scowling image and set it on a rock, in a solitary place, among the brambles: a phantom to frighten people.

My tutor, who knows he must fill his pupil's mind as much, or more, with affection as with reverence for virtue, will be able to tell him that the poets agree 690 with the common view, and to set his finger on the fact that the gods make men sweat harder in the approaches to the chambers of Venus than of Pallas. And when he begins to feel his oats, and the choice is offered him between Bradamante and Angelica as a mistress to be enjoyed—a natural, active, spirited, manly but not mannish beauty, next to a soft, affected,

5. Artificial words in scholastic logic whose vowels represent forms of syllogisms.

delicate, artificial beauty; one disguised as a boy,
wearing a shining helmet, the other dressed as a girl,
700 wearing a headdress of pearls—the tutor will think
his pupil manly even in love if he chooses quite
differently from that effeminate shepherd of Phrygia.[6]

He will teach him this new lesson, that the value
and height of true virtue lies in the ease, utility, and
pleasure of its practice, which is so far from being
difficult that children can master it as well as men,
the simple as well as the subtle. Virtue's tool is
moderation, not strength. Socrates, her prime favorite,
deliberately gives up his strength, to slip into the
710 naturalness and ease of her gait. She is the nursing
mother of human pleasures. By making them just,
she makes them sure and pure. By moderating them,
she keeps them in breath and appetite. By withdrawing
the ones she refuses, she makes us keener for the
ones she allows us; and she allows us abundantly
all those that nature wills, even to satiety, in maternal
fashion, if not to the point of lassitude (unless per-
chance we want to say that the regimen that stops
the drinker short of drunkenness, the eater short of
720 indigestion, the lecher short of baldness, is an enemy
of our pleasures). If she lacks the fortune of ordinary
men, she rises above it or does without it, and makes
herself a different sort of fortune that is all her own,
and no longer fluctuating and unsteady. She knows
how to be rich and powerful and learned, and lie
on perfumed mattresses. She loves life, she loves
beauty and glory and health. But her own particular
task is to know how to enjoy those blessings with
temperance, and to lose them with fortitude: a task
730 far more noble than harsh, without which the course
of any life is denatured, turbulent, and deformed,
and fit to be associated with those dangers, those

6. Paris, whose award of the golden apple, the prize of beauty,
to Aphrodite instead of Hera or Athene, led to the Trojan War.
Bradamante and Angelica are two heroines of Ariosto's *Orlando
Furioso*.

brambles, and those monsters....

For our boy, a closet, a garden, the table and the bed, solitude, company, morning and evening, all hours will be the same, all places will be his study; for philosophy, which, as the molder of judgment and conduct, will be his principal lesson, has this privilege of being everywhere at home....

Thus he will doubtless be less idle than others. But, 740 as the steps we take walking back and forth in a gallery, though there be three times as many, do not tire us like those we take on a set journey, so our lesson, occurring as if by chance, not bound to any time or place, and mingling with all our actions, will slip by without being felt. Even games and exercises will be a good part of his study: running, wrestling, ^Cmusic, ^Adancing, hunting, handling horses and weapons. I want his outward behavior and social grace ^Cand his physical adaptability ^Ato be fashioned at 750 the same time with his soul. It is not a soul that is being trained, not a body, but a man; these parts must not be separated. And, as Plato says, they must not be trained one without the other, but driven abreast like a pair of horses harnessed to the same pole. ^CAnd, to hear him, does he not seem to give more time and care to exercises of the body, and to think that the mind gets its exercise at the same time, and not the other way around?

^AFor the rest, this education is to be carried on 760 with severe gentleness, not as is customary. Instead of being invited to letters, children are shown in truth nothing but horror and cruelty. Away with violence and compulsion! There is nothing to my mind which so depraves and stupefies a wellborn nature. If you would like him to fear shame and chastisement, don't harden him to them. Harden him to sweat and cold, wind and sun, and the dangers that he must scorn; wean him from all softness and delicacy in dressing and sleeping, eating and drinking; accustom him to 770 everything. Let him not be a pretty boy and a little lady, but a lusty and vigorous youth.

^CAs a boy, a man, and a graybeard, I have always thought and judged in the same way. But, among other things, I have always disliked the discipline of most of our schools. They might have erred less harmfully by leaning toward indulgence. They are a real jail of captive youth. They make them slack, by punishing them for slackness before they show
780 it. Go in at lesson time: you hear nothing but cries, both from tortured boys and from masters drunk with rage. What a way to arouse zest for their lesson in these tender and timid souls, to guide them to it with a horrible scowl and hands armed with rods! Wicked and pernicious system! Besides, as Quintilian very rightly remarked, this imperious authority brings on dangerous consequences, and especially in our manner of punishment. How much more fittingly would their classes be strewn with flowers and leaves than with
790 bloody stumps of birch rods! I would have portraits there of Joy and Gladness, and Flora and the Graces, as the philosopher Speusippus had in his school. Where their profit is, let their frolic be also. Healthy foods should be sweetened for the child, and harmful ones dipped in gall.

It is wonderful how solicitous Plato shows himself in his *Laws* about the gaiety and pastimes of the youth of his city, and how much he dwells upon their races, games, songs, jumping, and dancing, whose conduct
800 and patronage he says antiquity gave to the gods themselves: Apollo, the Muses, and Minerva. He extends this to a thousand precepts for his gymnasiums; as for the literary studies, he wastes little time on them, and seems to recommend poetry in particular only for the sake of the music.

^AAny strangeness and peculiarity in our conduct and ways is to be avoided as inimical to social intercourse, ^Cand unnatural. Who would not be astonished at the constitution of Demophon, Alexander's
810 steward, who sweated in the shade and shivered in the sun? ^AI have seen men flee from the smell of apples more than from harquebus fire, others take

fright at a mouse, others throw up at the sight of cream, and others at the plumping of a feather bed; and Germanicus could not endure either the sight or the crowing of cocks. There may perhaps be some occult quality in this; but a man could exterminate it, in my opinion, if he set about it early. Education has won this much from me—it is true that it was not without some trouble—that, except for beer, my 820 appetite adapts itself indiscriminately to everything people eat.

While the body is still supple, it should for that reason be bent to all fashions and customs. And provided his appetite and will can be kept in check, let a young man boldly be made fit for all nations and companies, even for dissoluteness and excess, if need be. ^CLet his training follow usage. ^ALet him be able to do all things, and love to do only the good. The philosophers themselves do not think it praise- 830 worthy in Callisthenes to have lost the good graces of his master Alexander the Great by refusing to keep pace with him in drinking. He will laugh, he will carouse, he will dissipate with his prince. Even in dissipation I want him to outdo his comrades in vigor and endurance; and I want him to refrain from doing evil, not for lack of power or knowledge, but for lack of will. ^C*There is a great difference between not wishing to do evil and not knowing how* [Seneca]....

Going to Orléans one day, I met, in that plain this 840 side of Cléry, two teachers coming to Bordeaux, about fifty yards apart. Further off, behind them, I perceived a company and a lord at the head, who was the late Count de La Rochefoucauld. One of my men inquired of the first of these teachers who was the gentleman that came behind him. He, not having seen the retinue that was following him, and thinking that my man was talking about his companion, replied comically: "He is not a gentleman; he is a grammarian, and I am a logician."   850

Now, we who are trying on the contrary to make not a grammarian or a logician, but a gentleman, let

us allow them to misuse their free time; we have business elsewhere. Provided our pupil is well equipped with substance, words will follow only too readily; if they won't follow willingly, he will drag them. I hear some making excuses for not being able to express themselves, and pretending to have their heads full of many fine things, but to be unable to
860 express them for lack of eloquence. That is all bluff. Do you know what I think those things are? They are shadows that come to them of some shapeless conceptions, which they cannot untangle and clear up within, and consequently cannot set forth without: they do not understand themselves yet. And just watch them stammer on the point of giving birth; you will conclude that they are laboring not for delivery, but ^Cfor conception, and ^Athat they are only trying to lick into shape this unfinished matter. For my part
870 I hold, ^Cand Socrates makes it a rule, ^Athat whoever has a vivid and clear idea in his mind will express it, if necessary in Bergamask dialect, or, if he is dumb, by signs:

Master the stuff, and words will freely follow.

HORACE

And as another said just as poetically in his prose: *When things have taken possession of the mind, words come thick and fast* [Seneca]. ^CAnd another: *The things themselves carry the words along* [Cicero].
880 ^AHe knows no ablatives, conjunctives, substantives, or grammar; nor does his lackey, or a fishwife of the Petit Pont, and yet they will talk your ear off, if you like, and will perhaps stumble as little over the rules of their language as the best master of arts in France. He does not know rhetoric, or how in a preface to capture the benevolence of the gentle reader; nor does he care to know it. In truth, all this fine painting is easily eclipsed by the luster of a simple natural truth....
890 True, but what will he do if someone presses him with the sophistic subtlety of some syllogism? "Ham

makes us drink; drinking quenches thirst; therefore ham quenches thirst." ^CLet him laugh at it; it is subtler to laugh at it than to answer it.

Let him borrow from Aristippus this amusing counterthrust: "Why shall I untie it, since it gives me so much trouble tied?" Someone was using dialectical tricks against Cleanthes, when Chrysippus said to him: "Play those tricks with children, and don't divert the thoughts of a grown man to that stuff." ^AIf those 900 silly quibbles, ^C*tortuous and thorny sophisms* [Cicero], ^Aare intended to convince him of a lie, that is dangerous; but if they remain without effect and only make him laugh, I do not see why he need be on his guard against them.

There are some men so stupid that they go a mile out of their way to chase after a fine word, ^C*or who do not fit words to things, but seek irrelevant things which their words may fit* [Quintilian]. And as another says, *There are some who are led by the charm of* 910 *some attractive word to write something they had not intended* [Seneca]. I much more readily twist a good saying to sew it on me than I twist the thread of my thought to go and fetch it. ^AOn the contrary, it is for words to serve and follow; and let Gascon get there if French cannot. I want the substance to stand out, and so to fill the imagination of the listener that he will have no memory of the words. The speech I love is a simple, natural speech, the same on paper as in the mouth; a speech succulent and sinewy, brief 920 and compressed, ^Cnot so much dainty and well-combed as vehement and brusque:

The speech that strikes the mind will have most taste;

EPITAPH OF LUCAN

^Arather difficult than boring, remote from affectation, irregular, disconnected and bold; each bit making a body in itself; not pedantic, not monkish, not lawyer-like, but rather soldierly, as Suetonius calls Julius Caesar's speech; ^Cand yet I do not quite see why he calls it so.   930

There is no doubt that Greek and Latin are great and handsome ornaments, but we buy them too dear. I shall tell you here a way to get them cheaper than usual, which was tried out on myself. Anyone who wants to can use it.

My late father, having made all the inquiries a man can make, among men of learning and understanding, about a superlative system of education, became aware of the drawbacks that were prevalent; and he was
940 told that the long time we put into learning languages ^Cwhich cost the ancient Greeks and Romans nothing ^Awas the only reason we could not attain their greatness in soul and in knowledge. I do not think that that is the only reason. At all events, the expedient my father hit upon was this, that while I was nursing and before the first loosening of my tongue, he put me in the care of a German, who has since died a famous doctor in France, wholly ignorant of our language and very well versed in Latin.[7] This man,
950 whom he had sent for expressly, and who was very highly paid, had me constantly in his hands. There were also two others with him, less learned, to attend me and relieve him. These spoke to me in no other language than Latin. As for the rest of my father's household, it was an inviolable rule that neither my father himself, nor my mother, nor any valet or housemaid, should speak anything in my presence but such Latin words as each had learned in order to jabber with me.
960   It is wonderful how everyone profited from this. My father and mother learned enough Latin in this way to understand it, and acquired sufficient skill to use it when necessary, as did also the servants who were most attached to my service. Altogether, we Latinized ourselves so much that it overflowed all the way to our villages on every side, where there still remain several Latin names for artisans and tools

7. Doctor Horstanus, later a professor at the Collège de Guyenne at Bordeaux.

that have taken root by usage. As for me, I was over six before I understood any more French or Perigordian than Arabic. And without artificial means, without 970 a book, without grammar or precept, without the whip and without tears, I had learned a Latin quite as pure as what my schoolmaster knew, for I could not have contaminated or altered it. If as a test they wanted to give me a theme in the school fashion, where they give it to others in French, they had to give it to me in bad Latin, to turn it into good. And Nicholas Grouchy, who wrote *De Comitiis Romanorum,* Guillaume Guerente, who wrote a commentary on Aristotle, George Buchanan, that great Scottish poet, 980 [B]Marc-Antoine Muret, [C]whom France and Italy recognize as the best orator of his time, [A]my private tutors, have often told me that in my childhood I had that language so ready and handy that they were afraid to accost me. Buchanan, whom I afterward saw in the suite of the late Marshal de Brissac, told me that he was writing on the education of children and that he was taking my education as a model; for he was then in charge of that Count de Brissac who later showed himself so valorous and brave.   990

As for Greek, of which I have practically no knowledge at all, my father planned to have me taught it artificially, but in a new way, in the form of amusement and exercise. We volleyed our conjugations back and forth, like those who learn arithmetic and geometry by such games as checkers and chess. For among other things he had been advised to teach me to enjoy knowledge and duty by my own free will and desire, and to educate my mind in all gentleness and freedom, without rigor and constraint. He did this so religiously 1000 that because some hold that it troubles the tender brains of children to wake them in the morning with a start, and to snatch them suddenly and violently from their sleep, in which they are plunged much more deeply than we are, he had me awakened by the sound of some instrument; and I was never without a man to do this for me.

This example will be enough to let you judge the rest, and also to commend both the prudence and
1010 the affection of so good a father, who is not at all to be blamed if he reaped no fruit corresponding to such an excellent cultivation. Two things were the cause of this: first, the sterile and unfit soil; for though my health was sound and complete and my nature gentle and tractable, I was withal so sluggish, lax, and drowsy that they could not tear me from my sloth, not even to make me play. What I saw, I saw well, and beneath this inert appearance nourished bold ideas and opinions beyond my years. I had a slow
1020 mind, which would go only as far as it was led; a tardy understanding, a weak imagination, and on top of all an incredible lack of memory. It is no wonder if he could get nothing worth while from all this.

Second, just as people frantically eager to be cured will try any sort of advice, that good man, being extremely afraid of failing in a thing so close to his heart, at last let himself be carried away by the common opinion, which always follows the leader like a flock of cranes, and fell in line with custom, having no
1030 longer about him the men who had given him those first plans, which he had brought from Italy. And he sent me, when I was about six, to the Collège de Guyenne, which was then very flourishing and the best in France. And there, nothing could be added to the care he took, both to choose me competent personal tutors and in all the other aspects of my education, in which he held out for certain particular practices contrary to school usage. But for all that, it was still school. My Latin promptly degenerated,
1040 and since then, for lack of practice, I have lost all use of it. And all this novel education of mine did for me was to make me skip immediately to the upper classes; for when I left the school at thirteen, I had finished my course (as they call it), and in truth without any benefit that I can place in evidence now....

ᴬTo return to my subject, there is nothing like arousing appetite and affection; otherwise all you make out of them is asses loaded with books. By dint of whipping, they are given their pocketful of learning for safekeeping; but if learning is to do us any good, 1050 we must not merely lodge it within us, we must espouse it.

It Is Folly to Measure the True and False by Our Own Capacity[1]

^APerhaps it is not without reason that we attribute facility in belief and conviction to simplicity and ignorance; for it seems to me I once learned that belief was a sort of impression made on our mind, and that the softer and less resistant the mind, the easier it was to imprint something on it. ^C*As the scale of the balance must necessarily sink under the weight placed upon it, so must the mind yield to evident things* [Cicero]. The more a mind is empty and without
10 counterpoise, the more easily it gives beneath the weight of the first persuasive argument. ^AThat is why children, common people, women, and sick people are most subject to being led by the ears. But then, on the other hand, it is foolish presumption to go around disdaining and condemning as false whatever does not seem likely to us; which is an ordinary vice in those who think they have more than common ability. I used to do so once; and if I heard of returning spirits, prognostications of future events, enchant-
20 ments, sorcery, or some other story that I could not swallow,

> Dreams, witches, miracles, magic alarms,
> Nocturnal specters, and Thessalian charms,
>
> HORACE

I felt compassion for the poor people who were taken in by these follies. And now I think that I was at least as much to be pitied myself. Not that experience

---

1. Chapter 27.

has since shown me anything surpassing my first
beliefs, and that through no fault of my curiosity;
but reason has taught me that to condemn a thing 30
thus, dogmatically, as false and impossible, is to
assume the advantage of knowing the bounds and
limits of God's will and of the power of our mother
Nature; and that there is no more notable folly in
the world than to reduce these things to the measure
of our capacity and competence. If we call prodigies
or miracles whatever our reason cannot reach, how
many of these appear continually to our eyes! Let
us consider through what clouds and how gropingly
we are led to the knowledge of most of the things 40
that are in our hands; assuredly we shall find that
it is rather familiarity than knowledge that takes away
their strangeness,

ᴮ But no one now, so tired of seeing are our eyes,
  Deigns to look up at the bright temples of the skies,

                                                    LUCRETIUS

ᴬ and that if those things were presented to us for
the first time, we should find them as incredible as
any others, or more so.

If they were here for the first time for men to see,   50
If they were set before us unexpectedly,
Nothing more marvelous than these things could be told,
Nothing more unbelievable for men of old.

                                                    LUCRETIUS

He who had never seen a river thought that the
first one he came across was the ocean. And the
things that are the greatest within our knowledge we
judge to be the utmost that nature can do in that
category.

ᴮ A fair-sized stream seems vast to one who until then   60
  Has never seen a greater; so with trees, with men.
ᴬ In every field each man regards as vast in size
  The greatest objects that have come before his eyes.

                                                    LUCRETIUS

^C*The mind becomes accustomed to things by the
habitual sight of them, and neither wonders nor inquires
about the reasons for the things it sees all the time*
[Cicero]....

The novelty of things incites us more than their
70 greatness to seek their causes.

^AWe must judge with more reverence the infinite
power of nature, and with more consciousness of our
ignorance and weakness. How many things of slight
probability there are, testified to by trustworthy people, which, if we cannot be convinced of them, we
should at least leave in suspense! For to condemn
them as impossible is to pretend, with rash presump-
tion, to know the limits of possibility. ^CIf people rightly
understood the difference between the impossible and
80 the unusual, and between what is contrary to the
orderly course of nature and what is contrary to the
common opinion of men, neither believing rashly nor
disbelieving easily, they would observe the rule of
"nothing too much," enjoined by Chilo.

^AWhen we find in Froissart that the count of Foix,
in Béarn, learned of the defeat of King John of Castile
at Juberoth the day after it happened, and the way
he says he learned it, we can laugh at it; and also
at the story our annals tell, that Pope Honorius
90 performed public funeral rites for King Philip Augustus
and commanded them to be performed throughout
Italy on the very day he died ^Bat Mantes. ^AFor the
authority of these witnesses has perhaps not enough
rank to keep us in check. But if Plutarch, besides
several examples that he cites from antiquity, says
that he knows with certain knowledge that in the time
of Domitian, the news of the battle lost by Antonius
in Germany was published in Rome, several days'
journey from there, and dispersed throughout the
100 whole world, on the same day it was lost; and if
Caesar maintains that it has often happened that the
report has preceded the event—shall we say that these
simple men let themselves be hoaxed like the common
herd, because they were not clear-sighted like our-

selves? Is there anything more delicate, clearer, and more alert than Pliny's judgment, when he sees fit to bring it into play, or anything farther from inanity? Leaving aside the excellence of his knowledge, which I count for less, in which of these qualities do we surpass him? However, there is no schoolboy so young 110 but he will convict him of falsehood, and want to give him a lesson on the progress of nature's works.

When we read in Bouchet about the miracles done by the relics of Saint Hilary, let it go: his credit is not great enough to take away our right to contradict him. But to condemn wholesale all similar stories seems to me a singular impudence. The great Saint Augustine testifies that he saw a blind child recover his sight upon the relics of Saint Gervase and Saint Protasius at Milan; a woman at Carthage cured of 120 a cancer by the sign of the cross that a newly baptized woman made over her; Hesperius, a close friend of his, cast out the spirits that infested his house with a little earth from the sepulcher of our Lord, and a paralytic promptly cured by this earth, later, when it had been carried to church; a woman in a procession, having touched Saint Stephen's shrine with a bouquet, and rubbed her eyes with this bouquet, recover her long-lost sight; and he reports many other miracles at which he says he himself was present. Of what 130 shall we accuse both him and two holy bishops, Aurelius and Maximinus, whom he calls upon as his witnesses? Shall it be of ignorance, simplicity, and credulity, or of knavery and imposture? Is there any man in our time so impudent that he thinks himself comparable to them, either in virtue and piety, or in learning, judgment, and ability? ^C *Who, though they brought forth no proof, might crush me by their mere authority* [Cicero].

^AIt is a dangerous and fateful presumption, besides 140 the absurd temerity that it implies, to disdain what we do not comprehend. For after you have established, according to your fine understanding, the limits of truth and falsehood, and it turns out that you must

necessarily believe things even stranger than those you deny, you are obliged from then on to abandon these limits. Now, what seems to me to bring as much disorder into our consciences as anything, in these religious troubles that we are in, is this partial surrender
150 of their beliefs by Catholics. It seems to them that they are being very moderate and understanding when they yield to their opponents some of the articles in dispute. But, besides the fact that they do not see what an advantage it is to a man charging you for you to begin to give ground and withdraw, and how much that encourages him to pursue his point, those articles which they select as the most trivial are sometimes very important. We must either submit completely to the authority of our ecclesiastical gov-
160 ernment, or do without it completely. It is not for us to decide what portion of obedience we owe it.

Moreover, I can say this for having tried it. In other days I exercised this freedom of personal choice and selection, regarding with negligence certain points in the observance of our Church which seem more vain or strange than others; until, coming to discuss them with learned men, I found that these things have a massive and very solid foundation, and that it is only stupidity and ignorance that make us receive
170 them with less reverence than the rest. Why do we not remember how much contradiction we sense even in our own judgment? How many things were articles of faith to us yesterday, which are fables to us today? Vainglory and curiosity are the two scourges of our soul. The latter leads us to thrust our noses into everything, and the former forbids us to leave anything unresolved and undecided.

BOOK II

Of the Inconsistency
of Our Actions [1]

^AThose who make a practice of comparing human actions are never so perplexed as when they try to see them as a whole and in the same light; for they commonly contradict each other so strangely that it seems impossible that they have come from the same shop. One moment young Marius is a son of Mars, another moment a son of Venus. Pope Boniface VIII, they say, entered office like a fox, behaved in it like a lion, and died like a dog. And who would believe that it was Nero, that living image of cruelty, who 10 said, when they brought him in customary fashion the sentence of a condemned criminal to sign: "Would to God I had never learned to write!" So much his heart was wrung at condemning a man to death!

Everything is so full of such examples—each man, in fact, can supply himself with so many—that I find it strange to see intelligent men sometimes going to great pains to match these pieces; seeing that irresolution seems to me the most common and apparent defect of our nature, as witness that famous line of 20 Publilius, the farce writer:

> Bad is the plan that never can be changed.
>
> PUBLILIUS SYRUS

^BThere is some justification for basing a judgment of a man on the most ordinary acts of his life; but in view of the natural instability of our conduct and opinions, it has often seemed to me that even good authors are wrong to insist on fashioning a consistent and solid fabric out of us. They choose one general characteristic, and go and arrange and interpret all 30

1. Chapter I.

41

a man's actions to fit their picture; and if they cannot
twist them enough, they go and set them down to
dissimulation. Augustus has escaped them; for there
is in this man throughout the course of his life such
an obvious, abrupt, and continual variety of actions
that even the boldest judges have had to let him go,
intact and unsolved. Nothing is harder for me than
to believe in men's consistency, nothing easier than
to believe in their inconsistency. He who would judge
40 them in detail ^Cand distinctly, bit by bit, ^Bwould more
often hit upon the truth.

^AIn all antiquity it is hard to pick out a dozen men
who set their lives to a certain and constant course,
which is the principal goal of wisdom. For, to comprise
all wisdom in a word, says an ancient [Seneca], and
to embrace all the rules of our life in one, it is "always
to will the same things, and always to oppose the
same things." I would not deign, he says, to add
"provided the will is just"; for if it is not just, it
50 cannot always be whole.

In truth, I once learned that vice is only unruliness
and lack of moderation, and that consequently consistency cannot be attributed to it. It is a maxim of
Demosthenes, they say, that the beginning of all virtue
is consultation and deliberation; and the end and
perfection, consistency. If it were by reasoning that
we settled on a particular course of action, we would
choose the fairest course—but no one has thought
of that:

60   He spurns the thing he sought, and seeks anew
       What he just spurned; he seethes, his life's askew.

                                        HORACE

Our ordinary practice is to follow the inclinations
of our appetite, to the left, to the right, uphill and
down, as the wind of circumstance carries us. We
think of what we want only at the moment we want
it, and we change like that animal which takes the
color of the place you set it on. What we have just
now planned, we presently change, and presently again

we retrace our steps: nothing but oscillation and   70
inconsistency:

> Like puppets we are moved by outside strings.
>
> HORACE

We do not go; we are carried away, like floating
objects, now gently, now violently, according as the
water is angry or calm:

> Do we not see all humans unaware
> And changing place, as if to drop the load they bear?
>
> LUCRETIUS

[A]Every day a new fancy, and our humors shift with   80
the shifts in the weather:

> Such are the minds of men, as is the fertile light
> That Father Jove himself sends down to make earth bright.
>
> HOMER

[C]We float between different states of mind; we
wish nothing freely, nothing absolutely, nothing constantly. [A]If any man could prescribe and establish
definite laws and a definite organization in his head,
we should see shining throughout his life an evenness
of habits, an order, and an infallible relation between   90
his principles and his practice.

[C]Empedocles noticed this inconsistency in the Agri-
gentines, that they abandoned themselves to pleasures
as if they were to die on the morrow, and built as
if they were never to die.

[A]This man[2] would be easy to understand, as is
shown by the example of the younger Cato: he who
has touched one chord of him has touched all; he
is a harmony of perfectly concordant sounds, which
cannot conflict. With us, it is the opposite: for so   100
many actions, we need so many individual judgments.
The surest thing, in my opinion, would be to trace
our actions to the neighboring circumstances, without

_____

2. The disciplined man in the sentence before last.

getting into any further research and without drawing from them any other conclusions.

During the disorders of our poor country,[3] I was told that a girl, living near where I then was, had thrown herself out of a high window to avoid the violence of a knavish soldier quartered in her house.
110 Not killed by the fall, she reasserted her purpose by trying to cut her throat with a knife. From this she was prevented, but only after wounding herself gravely. She herself confessed that the soldier had as yet pressed her only with requests, solicitations, and gifts; but she had been afraid, she said, that he would finally resort to force. And all this with such words, such expressions, not to mention the blood that testified to her virtue, as would have become another Lucrece.

Now, I learned that as a matter of fact, both before
120 and since, she was a wench not so hard to come to terms with. As the story says: Handsome and gentlemanly as you may be, when you have had no luck, do not promptly conclude that your mistress is inviolably chaste; for all you know, the mule driver may get his will with her.

Antigonus, having taken a liking to one of his soldiers for his virtue and valor, ordered his physicians to treat the man for a persistent internal malady that had long tormented him. After his cure, his master
130 noticed that he was going about his business much less warmly, and asked him what had changed him so and made him such a coward. "You yourself, Sire," he answered, "by delivering me from the ills that made my life indifferent to me." A soldier of Lucullus who had been robbed of everything by the enemy made a bold attack on them to get revenge. When he had retrieved his loss, Lucullus, having formed a good opinion of him, urged him to some dangerous exploit with all the fine expostulations he could think
140 of,

3. The religious civil wars between Catholics and Protestants, which lasted intermittently from 1562 to 1594.

With words that might have stirred a coward's heart.
HORACE

"Urge some poor soldier who has been robbed to do it," he replied;

Though but a rustic lout,
"That man will go who's lost his money," he called out;
HORACE

and resolutely refused to go.

^CWe read that Sultan Mohammed outrageously berated Hassan, leader of his Janissaries, because he 150 saw his troops giving way to the Hungarians and Hassan himself behaving like a coward in the fight. Hassan's only reply was to go and hurl himself furiously—alone, just as he was, arms in hand—into the first body of enemies that he met, by whom he was promptly swallowed up; this was perhaps not so much self-justification as a change of mood, nor so much his natural valor as fresh spite.

^AThat man whom you saw so adventurous yesterday, do not think it strange to find him just as cowardly 160 today: either anger, or necessity, or company, or wine, or the sound of a trumpet, had put his heart in his belly. His was a courage formed not by reason, but by one of these circumstances; it is no wonder if he has now been made different by other, contrary circumstances.

^CThese supple variations and contradictions that are seen in us have made some imagine that we have two souls, and others that two powers accompany us and drive us, each in its own way, one toward 170 good, the other toward evil; for such sudden diversity cannot well be reconciled with a simple subject.

^BNot only does the wind of accident move me at will, but, besides, I am moved and disturbed as a result merely of my own unstable posture; and anyone who observes carefully can hardly find himself twice in the same state. I give my soul now one face, now another, according to which direction I turn it. If I

speak of myself in different ways, that is because
180 I look at myself in different ways. All contradictions
may be found in me by some twist and in some fashion.
Bashful, insolent; ^Cchaste, lascivious; ^Btalkative, taci-
turn; tough, delicate; clever, stupid; surly, affable;
lying, truthful; ^Clearned, ignorant; liberal, miserly, and
prodigal: ^Ball this I see in myself to some extent
according to how I turn; and whoever studies himself
really attentively finds in himself, yes, even in his
judgment, this gyration and discord. I have nothing
to say about myself absolutely, simply, and solidly,
190 without confusion and without mixture, or in one word.
Distinguo is the most universal member of my logic.
   ^AAlthough I am always minded to say good of what
is good, and inclined to interpret favorably anything
that can be so interpreted, still it is true that the
strangeness of our condition makes it happen that
we are often driven to do good by vice itself—were
it not that doing good is judged by intention alone.

   Therefore one courageous deed must not be taken
to prove a man valiant; a man who was really valiant
200 would be so always and on all occasions. If valor
were a habit of virtue, and not a sally, it would make
a man equally resolute in any contingency, the same
alone as in company, the same in single combat as
in battle; for, whatever they say, there is not one
valor for the pavement and another for the camp.
As bravely would he bear an illness in his bed as
a wound in camp, and he would fear death no more
in his home than in an assault. We would not see
the same man charging into the breach with brave
210 assurance, and later tormenting himself, like a woman,
over the loss of a lawsuit or a son. ^CWhen, though
a coward against infamy, he is firm against poverty;
when, though weak against the surgeon's knives, he
is steadfast against the enemy's swords, the action
is praiseworthy, not the man.

   Many Greeks, says Cicero, cannot look at the
enemy, and are brave in sickness; the Cimbrians and
Celtiberians, just the opposite; *for nothing can be*

uniform that does not spring from a firm principle
[Cicero].   220
 ᴮThere is no more extreme valor of its kind than
Alexander's; but it is only of one kind, and not
complete and universal enough. ᶜIncomparable though
it is, it still has its blemishes; ᴮwhich is why we see
him worry so frantically when he conceives the slight-
est suspicion that his men are plotting against his life,
and why he behaves in such matters with such violent
and indiscriminate injustice and with a fear that
subverts his natural reason. Also superstition, with
which he was so strongly tainted, bears some stamp   230
of pusillanimity. ᶜAnd the excessiveness of the pen-
ance he did for the murder of Clytus is also evidence
of the unevenness of his temper.
 ᴬOur actions are nothing but a patchwork—ᶜ*they
despise pleasure, but are too cowardly in pain; they
are indifferent to glory, but infamy breaks their spirit*
[Cicero]—ᴬand we want to gain honor under false
colors. Virtue will not be followed except for her
own sake; and if we sometimes borrow her mask for
some other purpose, she promptly snatches it from   240
our face. It is a strong and vivid dye, once the soul
is steeped in it, and will not go without taking the
fabric with it. That is why, to judge a man, we must
follow his traces long and carefully. If he does not
maintain consistency for its own sake, ᶜ*with a way
of life that has been well considered and preconcerted*
[Cicero]; ᴬif changing circumstances make him
change his pace (I mean his path, for his pace may
be hastened or slowed), let him go: that man goes
before the wind, as the motto of our Talbot says.   250
 It is no wonder, says an ancient [Seneca], that
chance has so much power over us, since we live
by chance. A man who has not directed his life as
a whole toward a definite goal cannot possibly set
his particular actions in order. A man who does not
have a picture of the whole in his head cannot possibly
arrange the pieces. What good does it do a man to
lay in a supply of paints if he does not know what

he is to paint? No one makes a definite plan of his
260 life; we think about it only piecemeal. The archer must first know what he is aiming at, and then set his hand, his bow, his string, his arrow, and his movements for that goal. Our plans go astray because they have no direction and no aim. No wind works for the man who has no port of destination.

I do not agree with the judgment given in favor of Sophocles, on the strength of seeing one of his tragedies, that it proved him competent to manage his domestic affairs, against the accusation of his son.
270 ᶜNor do I think that the conjecture of the Parians sent to reform the Milesians was sufficient ground for the conclusion they drew. Visiting the island, they noticed the best-cultivated lands and the best-run country houses, and noted down the names of their owners. Then they assembled the citizens in the town and appointed these owners the new governors and magistrates, judging that they, who were careful of their private affairs, would be careful of those of the public.
280   ᴬWe are all patchwork, and so shapeless and diverse in composition that each bit, each moment, plays its own game. And there is as much difference between us and ourselves as between us and others. ᶜ*Consider it a great thing to play the part of one single man* [Seneca]. ᴬAmbition can teach men valor, and temperance, and liberality, and even justice. Greed can implant in the heart of a shop apprentice, brought up in obscurity and idleness, the confidence to cast himself far from hearth and home, in a frail boat
290 at the mercy of the waves and angry Neptune; it also teaches discretion and wisdom. Venus herself supplies resolution and boldness to boys still subject to discipline and the rod, and arms the tender hearts of virgins who are still in their mother's laps:

ᴮFurtively passing sleeping guards, with Love as guide,
Alone by night the girl comes to the young man's side.

TIBULLUS

^A In view of this, a sound intellect will refuse to judge
men simply by their outward actions; we must probe
the inside and discover what springs set men in motion. 300
But since this is an arduous and hazardous undertaking,
I wish fewer people would meddle with it.

Apology for
Raymond Sebond[1]

This chapter, by far the longest of the *Essays*, has been the most influential and remains one of the most perplexing. Its extreme skepticism, summed up in the famous motto *Que sçay-je?* (What do I know?), has been accepted by centuries of readers as the center of Montaigne's thought, although recent scholars have seen it rather as a step on his way to the psychological and moral convictions of Book III.

It is perplexing mainly because it belies its title. Sebond, whose "Natural Theology" Montaigne had translated at his father's request, had argued that man could learn all about God and religion by reading in the book of God's creation, the world. Montaigne shows his complete disagreement here, as he already had when he translated Sebond's Preface. He is the most apologetic of apologists. The best he can bring himself to say in the page or two that can be called a defense is that Sebond means well; that thanks to Sebond's faith (though by implication in spite of his method) the book may have some limited merit and use; and that anyway the bad state of religion in Montaigne's time shows that few men, if any, receive their religion in the right way.

Less than one-tenth of the chapter deals with Sebond at all. Primarily, it is a sustained argument of the impotence of unaided human reason, here set in the form of a counterattack against one group of objectors to Sebond and his book.

Understandably enough, the "Apology for Raymond Sebond" has given rise to varied interpretations. Some readers, like Sainte-Beuve, have seen in it a perfidious attack on Christianity; some argue that Montaigne merely forgot Sebond. The present translator prefers the theory that most of the chapter was written with no thought of Sebond, as a treatise on human presumption and the vanity of human reason; that the princess to whom Montaigne addresses his warning, almost certainly Margaret of Valois, asked him to defend the author he had translated; and that he built upon his attack on human reason a superstructure designed to make of it the best apology he could honestly make for his author.

The following plan is designed to show both the arrangement of the whole and the real importance of the various parts. The numbers opposite each part are the page-numbers in Volume II of Villey's 1930-1931 French edition of the *Essais*.

1. Chapter 12.

^AIn truth, knowledge is a great and very useful quality; those who despise it give evidence enough 80 of their stupidity. But yet I do not set its value at that extreme measure that some attribute to it, like Herillus the philosopher, who placed in it the sovereign good, and held that it was in its power to make us wise and content. That I do not believe, nor what

others have said, that knowledge is the mother of all virtue, and that all vice is produced by ignorance. If that is true, it is subject to a long interpretation.

90 My house has long been open to men of learning, and is well known to them. For my father, who ruled it for fifty years and more, inflamed with that new ardor with which King Francis I embraced letters and brought them into credit, sought with great diligence and expense the acquaintance of learned men, receiving them at his house like holy persons having some particular inspiration of divine wisdom, collecting their sayings and discourses like oracles, and with all the more reverence and religion as he was less qualified to judge them; for he had no knowledge of letters,

100 any more than his predecessors. Myself, I like them well enough, but I do not worship them.

Among others, Pierre Bunel, a man of great reputation for learning in his time, after staying a few days at Montaigne in the company of my father with other men of his sort, made him a present, on his departure, of a book entitled "Natural Theology, or Book of Creatures, by Master Raymond de Sabonde."[2] And because the Italian and Spanish languages were familiar to my father, and this book was composed in a

110 Spanish scrambled up with Latin endings, Bunel hoped that with a very little help he could make his profit of it; and recommended it to him as a very useful book and suited to the time in which he gave it to him; this was when the innovations of Luther were beginning to gain favor and to shake our old belief in many places.

In this he was very well advised, rightly foreseeing by rational inference that this incipient malady would easily degenerate into an execrable atheism. For the

120 common herd, not having the faculty of judging things in themselves, let themselves be carried away by

2. Raymond de Sebonde, Sebond, Sabaude, Sebeyde, Sabonde, etc., as his name is variously spelled, was a professor of medicine, theology, and philosophy at Toulouse around 1430. His "Natural Theology" was published in 1484.

chance and by appearances, when once they have
been given the temerity to despise and judge the
opinions that they had held in extreme reverence,
such as are those in which their salvation is concerned.
And when some articles of their religion have been
set in doubt and upon the balance, they will soon
after cast easily into like uncertainty all the other
parts of their belief, which had no more authority
or foundation in them than those that have been 130
shaken; and they shake off as a tyrannical yoke all
the impressions they had once received from the
authority of the laws or the reverence of ancient
usage—

^B For eagerly is trampled what once was too much feared

LUCRETIUS

—^A determined from then on to accept nothing to which
they have not applied their judgment and granted their
personal consent.

Now some days before his death, my father, having 140
by chance come across this book under a pile of other
abandoned papers, commanded me to put it into
French for him. It is nice to translate authors like
this one, where there is hardly anything but the matter
to reproduce; but those who have given much care
to grace and elegance of language are dangerous to
undertake, ^C especially to render them into a weaker
idiom.[3] ^A It was a very strange and a new occupation
for me; but being by chance at leisure at the time,
and being unable to disobey any command of the 150
best father there ever was, I got through it as best
I could; at which he was singularly pleased, and
ordered it to be printed; and this was done after his
death.

I found the ideas of this author fine, the arrangement and sequence of his work good, and his plan
full of piety. Because many people are busy reading
it, and especially the ladies, to whom we owe additional

3. French, which was still considered weaker than Latin.

help, I have often found myself in a position to help
160 them by clearing their book of two principal objections
that are made against it. His purpose is bold and
courageous, for he undertakes by human and natural
reasons to establish and prove against the atheists
all the articles of the Christian religion; wherein, to
tell the truth, I find him so firm and felicitous that
I do not think it is possible to do better in that argument,
and I think that no one has equaled him....

The first criticism that they make of his work is
that Christians do themselves harm in trying to support
170 their belief by human reasons, since it is conceived
only by faith and by a particular inspiration of divine
grace. In this objection there seems to be a certain
pious zeal, and for this reason we must try with all
the more mildness and respect to satisfy those who
advance it. This would be rather the task for a man
versed in theology than for myself, who know nothing
about it.

However, I think thus, that in a thing so divine
and so lofty, and so far surpassing human intelligence,
180 as is this truth with which it has pleased the goodness
of God to enlighten us, it is very necessary that he
still lend us his help, by extraordinary and privileged
favor, so that we may conceive it and lodge it in
us. And I do not think that purely human means are
at all capable of this; if they were, so many rare
and excellent souls, so abundantly furnished with
natural powers, in ancient times, would not have failed
to arrive at this knowledge through their reason. It
is faith alone that embraces vividly and surely the
190 high mysteries of our religion.

But this is not to say that it is not a very fine
and very laudable enterprise to accommodate also to
the service of our faith the natural and human tools
that God has given us. There can be no doubt that
this is the most honorable use that we could put them
to, and that there is no occupation or design more
worthy of a Christian man than to aim, by all his
studies and thoughts, to embellish, and amplify the

truth of his belief. We do not content ourselves with
serving God with mind and soul, we also owe and 200
render him a bodily reverence; we apply even our
limbs and movements and external things to honor
him. We must do the same here, and accompany our
faith with all the reason that is in us, but always
with this reservation, not to think that it is on us
that faith depends, or that our efforts and arguments
can attain a knowledge so supernatural and divine.

If it does not enter into us by an extraordinary
infusion; if it enters, I will not say only by reason,
but by human means of any sort, it is not in us in 210
its dignity or in its splendor. And yet I am afraid
that we enjoy it only in this way. If we held to God
by the mediation of a living faith, if we held to God
through him and not through ourselves, if we had
a divine foothold and foundation, human accidents
would not have the power to shake us as they do.
Our fort would not be prone to surrender to so weak
a battery; the love of novelty, the constraint of princes,
the good fortune of one party, a heedless and accidental
change in our opinions, would not have the power 220
to shake and alter our belief; we would not allow
it to be troubled by every new argument or by
persuasion, not even by all the rhetoric there ever
was; we should withstand those waves with inflexible
and immobile firmness,

> As a vast rock repels the dashing seas
> And sprays the roaring waves into the breeze
> With its great bulk.

AUTHOR UNKNOWN

If this ray of divinity touched us at all, it would appear 230
all over: not only our words, but also our works would
bear its light and luster. Everything that came from
us would be seen to be illuminated by this noble
brightness. We ought to be ashamed that in human
sects there never was a partisan, whatever difficult
and strange thing his doctrine maintained, who did
not to some extent conform his conduct and his life

to it; and so divine and celestial a teaching as ours
marks Christians only by their words.
240   B Do you want to see this? Compare our morals
with a Mohammedan's, or a pagan's; we always fall
short of them. Whereas, in view of the advantage
of our religion, we should shine with excellence at
an extreme and incomparable distance, and people
ought to say: "Are they so just, so charitable, so
good? Then they are Christians.".

See the horrible impudence with which we bandy
divine reasons about, and how irreligiously we have
both rejected them and taken them again, according
250 as fortune has changed our place in these public storms.
This proposition, so solemn, whether it is lawful for
a subject to rebel and take arms against his prince
in defense of religion—remember in whose mouths,
this year just past, the affirmative of this was the
buttress of one party, the negative was the buttress
of what other party; and hear now from what quarter
comes the voice and the instruction of both sides,
and whether the weapons make less din for this cause
than for that.[4] And we burn the people who say that
260 truth must be made to endure the yoke of our need.
And how much worse France does than say it!

A Let us confess the truth: if anyone should sift
out of the army, even the average loyalist army, those
who march in it from the pure zeal of affection for
religion, and also those who consider only the protec-
tion of the laws of their country or the service of
their prince, he could not make up one complete
company of men-at-arms out of them. Whence comes
this, that there are so few who have maintained the
270 same will and the same pace in our public movements,
and that we see them now going only at a walk, now
riding with free rein, and the same men now spoiling
our affairs by their violence and asperity, now by

4. Before the death of the Catholic king Henry III, assassinated
in 1589, the Protestants claimed the right to revolt, and the Catholics
denied it. When the Protestant king Henry IV succeeded Henry
III, both parties did an about-face.

their coolness, sluggishness, and heaviness, if it is
not that they are driven to it by private ^Cand accidental
^Aconsiderations according to whose diversity they are
stirred?

^CI see this evident, that we willingly accord to piety
only the services that flatter our passions. There is
no hostility that excels Christian hostility. Our zeal 280
does wonders when it is seconding our leaning toward
hatred, cruelty, ambition, avarice, detraction, rebel-
lion. Against the grain, toward goodness, benignity,
moderation, unless as by a miracle some rare nature
bears it, it will neither walk nor fly.

Our religion is made to extirpate vices; it covers
them, fosters them, incites them.

^AWe must not give God chaff for wheat, as they
say. If we believed in him, I do not say by faith,
but with a simple belief; in fact (and I say it to our 290
great confusion), if we believed in him just as in any
other history, if we knew him like one of our comrades,
we would love him above all other things, for the
infinite goodness and beauty that shines in him. At
least he would march in the same rank in our affection
as riches, pleasures, glory, and our friends.

^CThe best of us does not fear to outrage him as
he fears to outrage his neighbor, his kinsman, his
master. Is there any mind so simple that, having on
one side the object of one of our vicious pleasures 300
and on the other in equal knowledge and conviction
the state of immortal glory, he would trade the one
for the other? And yet we often renounce immortal
glory out of pure disdain; for what taste leads us
to blaspheme, unless perhaps the very taste of the
offense?...

All this is a very evident sign that we receive our
religion only in our own way and with our own hands,
and not otherwise than as other religions are received.
We happen to have been born in a country where 310
it was in practice; or we regard its antiquity or the
authority of the men who have maintained it; or we
fear the threats it fastens upon unbelievers, or pursue

its promises. Those considerations should be employed in our belief, but as subsidiaries; they are human ties. Another region, other witnesses, similar promises and threats, might imprint upon us in the same way a contrary belief.

[B]We are Christians by the same title that we are
320 Perigordians or Germans....

I have already, without thinking about it, half involved myself in the second objection which I had proposed to answer for Sebond.

Some say that his arguments are weak and unfit to prove what he proposes, and undertake to shatter them with ease. These must be shaken up a little more roughly, for they are more dangerous and malicious than the others. [C]People are prone to apply the meaning of other men's writings to suit opinions
330 that they have previously determined in their minds; and an atheist flatters himself by reducing all authors to atheism, infecting innocent matter with his own venom. [A]These men have some prepossession in judgment that makes their taste jaded for Sebond's reasons. Furthermore, it seems to them that they are given an easy game when set at liberty to combat our religion by purely human weapons, which they would not dare attack in its authoritative and commanding majesty.
340 The means I take to beat down this frenzy, and which seems fittest to me, is to crush and trample underfoot human arrogance and pride; to make them feel the inanity, the vanity and nothingness, of man; to wrest from their hands the puny weapons of their reason; to make them bow their heads and bite the ground beneath the authority and reverence of divine majesty. It is to this alone that knowledge and wisdom belong; it alone that can have some self-esteem, and from which we steal what we account and prize
350 ourselves for:

For God allows great thoughts to no one else.

HERODOTUS

CLet us beat down this presumption, the first foundation of the tyranny of the evil spirit. *For God resisteth the proud, and giveth grace to the humble* [Saint Peter]. Intelligence is in all gods, says Plato, and in very few men.

ANow it is nevertheless a great consolation to the Christian to see our frail mortal tools so properly suited to our holy and divine faith, that when they 360 are used on subjects that are by their nature frail and mortal, they are no more completely and power-fully appropriate. Let us see then if man has within his power other reasons more powerful than those of Sebond, or indeed if it is in him to arrive at any certainty by argument and reason....

AWhat does truth preach to us, when she exhorts us to flee worldly philosophy, when she so often inculcates in us that our wisdom is but folly before God; that of all vanities the vainest is man; that the 370 man who is presumptuous of his knowledge does not yet know what knowledge is; and that man, who is nothing, if he thinks he is something, seduces and deceives himself? These statements of the Holy Spirit express so clearly and so vividly what I wish to maintain, that no other proof would be needed against men who would surrender with all submission and obedience to its authority. But these men insist on being whipped to their own cost and will not allow us to combat their reason except by itself.   380

Let us then consider for the moment man alone, without outside assistance, armed solely with his own weapons, and deprived of divine grace and knowledge, which is his whole honor, his strength, and the founda-tion of his being. Let us see how much presence he has in this fine array....

APresumption is our natural and original malady. The most vulnerable and frail of all creatures is man, and at the same time the most arrogant. He feels and sees himself lodged here, amid the mire and dung 390 of the world, nailed and riveted to the worst, the deadest, and the most stagnant part of the universe,

on the lowest story of the house and the farthest from the vault of heaven, with the animals of the worst condition of the three;[5] and in his imagination he goes planting himself above the circle of the moon, and bringing the sky down beneath his feet. It is by the vanity of this same imagination that he equals himself to God, attributes to himself divine charac-
400 teristics, picks himself out and separates himself from the horde of other creatures, carves out their shares to his fellows and companions the animals, and distributes among them such portions of faculties and powers as he sees fit. How does he know, by the force of his intelligence, the secret internal stirrings of animals? By what comparison between them and us does he infer the stupidity that he attributes to them?

[C]When I play with my cat, who knows if I am
410 not a pastime to her more than she is to me?[6]...

I have said all this to maintain this resemblance that exists to human things. and to bring us back and join us to the majority. We are neither above nor below the rest: all that is under heaven, says the sage, incurs the same law and the same fortune,

[B] All things are bound by their own chains of fate.

LUCRETIUS

[A]There is some difference, there are orders and degrees; but it is under the aspect of one and the
420 same nature:

[B] And all things go their own way, nor forget
Distinctions by the law of nature set.

LUCRETIUS

[A] Man must be constrained and forced into line inside the barriers of this order. The poor wretch is in no

5. Those that walk, those that fly, those that swim.
6. The 1595 edition adds: "We entertain each other with reciprocal monkey tricks. If I have my time to begin or to refuse, so has she hers.

position really to step outside them; he is fettered
and bound, he is subjected to the same obligation
as the other creatures of his class, and in a very
ordinary condition, without any real and essential
prerogative or preeminence. That which he accords 430
himself in his mind and in his fancy has neither body
nor taste. And if it is true that he alone of all the
animals has this freedom of imagination and this
unruliness in thought that represents to him what is,
what is not, what he wants, the false and the true,
it is an advantage that is sold him very dear, and
in which he has little cause to glory, for from it springs
the principal source of the ills that oppress him: sin,
disease, irresolution, confusion, despair.

So I say, to return to my subject, that there is 440
no apparent reason to judge that the beasts do by
natural and obligatory instinct the same things that
we do by our choice and cleverness. We must infer
from like results like faculties,[7] and consequently
confess that this same reason, this same method that
we have for working, is also that of the animals.[8]

ᴬThe participation that we have in the knowledge
of truth, whatever it may be, has not been acquired
by our own powers. God has taught us that clearly
enough by the witnesses that he has chosen from 450
the common people, simple and ignorant, to instruct
us in his admirable secrets. Our faith is not of our
own acquiring, it is a pure present of another's
liberality. It is not by reasoning or by our understanding
that we have received our religion; it is by external
authority and command. The weakness of our judgment helps us more in this than its strength, and our
blindness more than our clear-sightedness. It is by
the mediation of our ignorance more than of our
knowledge that we are learned with that divine learn- 460

7. The 1595 edition adds: "and from richer results, richer faculties."

8. The 1595 edition reads, instead of "is also that of the animals,"
"the animals have it also, or some better one."

ing. It is no wonder if our natural and earthly powers cannot conceive that supernatural and heavenly knowledge; let us bring to it nothing of our own but obedience and submission. For, as it is written, "I will destroy the wisdom of the wise, and will bring to nothing the understanding of the prudent. Where is the wise? where is the scribe? where is the disputer of this world? hath not God made foolish the wisdom of this world? For after that the world by wisdom

470 knew not God, it pleased God by the foolishness of preaching to save them that believe" [I Corinthians].

Yet must I see at last whether it is in the power of man to find what he seeks, and whether that quest that he has been making for so many centuries has enriched him with any new power and any solid truth.

I think he will confess to me, if he speaks in all conscience, that all the profit he has gained from so long a pursuit is to have learned to acknowledge his weakness. The ignorance that was naturally in us we

480 have by long study confirmed and verified.

To really learned men has happened what happens to ears of wheat: they rise high and lofty, heads erect and proud, as long as they are empty; but when they are full and swollen with grain in their ripeness, they begin to grow humble and lower their horns....

Our speech has its weaknesses and its defects, like all the rest. Most of the occasions for the troubles of the world are grammatical. Our lawsuits spring only from debate over the interpretation of the laws,

490 and most of our wars from the inability to express clearly the conventions and treaties of agreement of princes. How many quarrels, and how important, have been produced in the world by doubt of the meaning of that syllable *Hoc*![9]

[B]Let us take the sentence that logic itself offers us as the clearest. If you say "It is fine weather,"

9. Much of the dispute over transubstantiation, especially between Catholics and Protestants, centers on the interpretation of Christ's words: "Hoc est corpus meum . . ."

and if you are speaking the truth, then it is fine weather.
Isn't that a sure way of speaking? Still it will deceive
us. To show this let us continue the example. If you
say "I lie," and if you are speaking the truth, then 500
you lie. The art, the reason, the force, of the conclusion
of this one are the same as in the other; yet there
we are stuck in the mud.

^I can see why the Pyrrhonian philosophers cannot
express their general conception in any manner of
speaking; for they would need a new language. Ours
is wholly formed of affirmative propositions, which
to them are utterly repugnant; so that when they say
"I doubt," immediately you have them by the throat
to make them admit that at least they know and are 510
sure of this fact, that they doubt. Thus they have
been constrained to take refuge in this comparison
from medicine, without which their attitude would
be inexplicable: when they declare "I do not know"
or "I doubt," they say that this proposition carries
itself away with the rest, no more nor less than rhubarb,
which expels evil humors and carries itself off with
them.

This idea is more firmly grasped in the form of
interrogation: "What do I know?"[10]—the words I bear 520
as a motto, inscribed over a pair of scales....

^You,[11] for whom I have taken the pains to extend
so long a work contrary to my custom, will not shrink
from upholding your Sebond by the ordinary form
of argument in which you are instructed every day,
and in that you will exercise your mind and your
learning. For this final fencer's trick must not be
employed except as an extreme remedy. It is a desper-
ate stroke, in which you must abandon your weapons
to make your adversary lose his, and a secret trick 530
that must be used rarely and reservedly. It is great

10. The famous *"Que sçay-je?"* which many consider Montaigne's central idea.
11. This entire essay is addressed almost certainly to Margaret
of Valois, daughter of Henry II and Catherine de' Medici, and
wife of Henry of Navarre, the future Henry IV of France.

rashness to ruin yourself in order to ruin another....

^AHere we are shaking the barriers and last fences of knowledge, in which extremity is a vice, as in virtue. Stay on the highroad; it is no good to be so subtle and clever. Remember what the Tuscan proverb says: *He who grows too keen cuts himself* [Petrarch].

In your opinions and remarks, as well as in your conduct and everything else, I advise moderation and
540 temperance, and avoidance of novelty and strangeness. All eccentric ways irritate me. You who, by the authority that your greatness brings you, and still more by the advantages which the qualities that are more your own give you, can by the flicker of an eye command whomever you please, should have given this assignment to some professional man of letters, who would have supported and enriched this theme for you in quite another way. However, here is enough for your needs.
550 ·Epicurus used to say of the laws that the worst were so necessary that without them men would devour one another. ^CAnd Plato, very close, says that without laws we should live like brutish animals; and he tries to prove it.

^AOur mind is an erratic, dangerous, and heedless tool; it is hard to impose order and moderation upon it. And in my time those who have some rare excellence beyond the others, and some extraordinary quickness, are nearly all, we see, incontinent in the license of
560 their opinions and conduct. It is a miracle if you find a sedate and sociable one.

People are right to give the tightest possible barriers to the human mind....

I who spy on myself more closely, who have my eyes unceasingly intent on myself, as one who has not much business elsewhere—

> Quite without care
> What king, in frigid lands beneath the Bear,
> ᵗ⸱ feared, or what makes Tiridates quake

570   HORACE

—I would hardly dare tell of the vanity and weakness that I find in myself. My footing is so unsteady and so insecure, I find it so vacillating and ready to slip, and my sight is so unreliable, that on an empty stomach I feel myself another man than after a meal. If my health smiles upon me, and the brightness of a beautiful day, I am a fine fellow; if I have a corn bothering my toe, I am surly, unpleasant, and unapproachable. [B]One and the same pace of a horse seems to me now rough, now easy, and the same road at one time 580 shorter, another time longer, and one and the same shape now more, now less agreeable. [A]Now I am ready to do anything, now to do nothing; what is a pleasure to me at this moment will some time be a trouble. A thousand unconsidered and accidental impulses arise in me. Either the melancholic humor grips me, or the choleric; and at this moment sadness predominates in me by its own private authority, at that moment good cheer.

When I pick up books, I will have perceived in 590 such-and-such a passage surpassing charms which will have struck my soul; let me come upon it another time, in vain I turn it over and over, in vain I twist it and manipulate it, to me it is a shapeless and unrecognizable mass.

[B]Even in my own writings I do not always find again the sense of my first thought; I do not know what I meant to say, and often I get burned by correcting and putting in a new meaning, because I have lost the first one, which was better.   600

I do nothing but come and go. My judgment does not always go forward; it floats, it strays,

> Like a tiny boat,
> Caught by a raging wind on the vast sea.
>
> CATULLUS

Many times (as I sometimes do deliberately), having undertaken as exercise and sport to maintain an opinion contrary to my own, my mind, applying itself and turning in that direction, attaches me to it so firmly

610 that I can no longer find the reason for my former
opinion, and I abandon it. I draw myself along in
almost any direction I lean, whatever it may be, and
carry myself away by my own weight.

Nearly every man would say as much of himself,
if he considered himself as I do. Preachers know that
the emotion that comes to them as they talk incites
them toward belief; and that in anger we give ourselves
up more completely to the defense of our proposition,
imprint it on ourselves, and embrace it with more
620 vehemence and approval than we do in our cool and
sedate mood.

You recite a case simply to a lawyer, he answers
you wavering and doubtful, you feel that it is a matter
of indifference to him whether he undertakes to
support one party or the other. Have you paid him
well to get his teeth into it and get excited about
it, is he beginning to be involved in it, has he got
his will warmed up about it? His reason and his
knowledge are warmed up at the same time. Behold
630 an evident and indubitable truth that appears to his
intelligence. He discovers a wholly new light on your
case, and believes it in all conscience, and persuades
himself that it is so....

^CAnd here at home I have seen things which were
capital offenses among us become legitimate; and we
who consider other things legitimate are liable, according to the uncertainty of the fortunes of war,
to be one day guilty of human and divine high treason,
when our justice falls into the mercy of injustice,
640 and, after a few years of captivity, assumes a contrary
character.

How could that ancient god [12] more clearly accuse
human knowledge of ignorance of the divine being,
and teach men that religion was only a creature of
their own invention, suitable to bind their society
together, than by declaring, as he did, to those who

12. Apollo.

sought instruction therein at his tripod, that the true
cult for each man was that which he found observed
according to the practice of the place he was in?

O God, what an obligation do we not have to the 650
benignity of our sovereign creator for having freed
our belief from the folly of those vagabond and
arbitrary devotions, and having based it on the eternal
foundation of his holy word?

ᴬWhat then will philosophy tell us in this our need?
To follow the laws of our country—that is to say,
the undulating sea of the opinions of a people or a
prince, which will paint me justice in as many colors,
and refashion it into as many faces, as there are
changes of passion in those men? I cannot have my 660
judgment so flexible.

What am I to make of a virtue that I saw in credit
yesterday, that will be discredited tomorrow, ᶜand
that becomes a crime on the other side of the river?
What of a truth that is bounded by these mountains
and is falsehood to the world that lives beyond?...

ᴬNow, since our condition accommodates things
to itself and transforms them according to itself, we
no longer know what things are in truth; for nothing
comes to us except falsified and altered by our senses. 670
When the compass, the square, and the ruler are off,
all the proportions drawn from them, all the buildings
erected by their measure, are also necessarily imperfect
and defective. The uncertainty of our senses makes
everything they produce uncertain. . . . Furthermore,
who shall be fit to judge these differences? As we
say in disputes about religion that we need a judge
not attached to either party, free from preference and
passion, which is impossible among Christians, so it
is in this. For if he is old, he cannot judge the sense 680
perception of old age, being himself a party in this
dispute; if he is young, likewise; healthy, likewise;
likewise sick, asleep, or awake. We would need
someone exempt from all these qualities, so that with
an unprejudiced judgment he might judge of these

propositions as of things indifferent to him; and by that score we would need a judge that never was.

To judge the appearances that we receive of objects, we would need a judicatory instrument; to verify this instrument, we need a demonstration; to verify the demonstration, an instrument: there we are in a circle.

Since the senses cannot decide our dispute, being themselves full of uncertainty, it must be reason that does so. No reason can be established without another reason: there we go retreating back to infinity.

Our conception is not itself applied to foreign objects, but is conceived through the mediation of the senses; and the senses do not comprehend the foreign object, but only their own impressions. And thus the conception and semblance we form is not of the object, but only of the impression and effect made on the sense; which impression and the object are different things. Wherefore whoever judges by appearances judges by something other than the object.

And as for saying that the impressions of the senses convey to the soul the quality of the foreign objects by resemblance, how can the soul and understanding make sure of this resemblance, having of itself no communication with foreign objects? Just as a man who does not know Socrates, seeing his portrait, cannot say that it resembles him.

Now if anyone should want to judge by appearances anyway, to judge by all appearances is impossible, for they clash with one another by their contradictions and discrepancies, as we see by experience. Shall some selected appearances rule the others? We shall have to verify this selection by another selection, the second by a third; and thus it will never be finished.

Finally, there is no existence that is constant, either of our being or of that of objects. And we, and our judgment, and all mortal things go on flowing and rolling unceasingly. Thus nothing certain can be established about one thing by another, both the judging and the judged being in continual change and motion.

We have no communication with being,[13] because
every human nature is always midway between birth
and death, offering only a dim semblance and shadow
of itself, and an uncertain and feeble opinion. And
if by chance you fix your thought on trying to grasp   730
its essence, it will be neither more nor less than if
someone tried to grasp water: for the more he squeezes
and presses what by its nature flows all over, the
more he will lose what he was trying to hold and
grasp. Thus, all things being subject to pass from
one change to another, reason, seeking a real stability
in them, is baffled, being unable to apprehend anything
stable and permanent; because everything is either
coming into being and not yet fully existent, or
beginning to die before it is born. . . .   740
Our prime dies and passes when old age comes
along, and youth ends in the prime of the grown man,
childhood in youth, and infancy in childhood. And
yesterday dies in today, and today will die in tomorrow;
and there is nothing that abides and is always the
same.
For, to prove that this is so, if we always remain
one and the same, how is it that we rejoice now in
one thing, and now in another? How is it that we
love opposite things or hate them, praise them or   750
blame them? How do we have different affections,
no longer retaining the same feeling within the same
thought? For it is not plausible that we take up different
passions without changing; and what suffers change
does not remain one and the same, and if it is not
one and the same, it also *is* not; but together with
its *being the same,* it also changes its simple *being,*
from one thing always becoming another. And consequently the senses of nature are mistaken and lie,

13. All the passage that follows, down to the fourth paragraph
from the end of the essay, is copied almost word for word from
Plutarch's *Moral Essays,* "On the Meaning of εἰ," in the French
translation by Jacques Amyot.

760 taking what appears for what is, for want of really
knowing what it is that *is*.

But then what really is? That which is eternal: that
is to say, what never had birth, nor will ever have
an end; to which time never brings any change. For
time is a mobile thing, which appears as in a shadow,
together with matter, which is ever running and flowing, without ever remaining stable or permanent. To
which belong the words *before* and *after*, and *has
been* or *will be*, which at the very first sight show
770 very evidently that time is not a thing that *is*; for
it would be a great stupidity and a perfectly apparent
falsehood to say that that *is* which is not yet in being,
or which already has ceased to be. And as for these
words, *present, immediate, now*, on which it seems
that we chiefly found and support our understanding
of time, reason discovering this immediately destroys
it; for she at once splits and divides it into future
and past, as though wanting to see it necessarily divided
in two.
780   The same thing happens to nature that is measured,
as to time that measures it. For there is nothing in
it either that abides or is stable; but all things in it
are either born, or being born, or dying. For which
reason it would be a sin to say of God, who is the
only one that *is*, that he *was* or *will be*. For those
terms represent declinings, transitions, or vicissitudes
of what cannot endure or remain in being. Wherefore
we must conclude that God alone *is*—not at all
according to any measure of time, but according to
790 an eternity immutable and immobile, not measured
by time or subject to any decline; before whom there
is nothing, nor will there be after, nor is there anything
more new or more recent; but one who really is—who
by one single *now* fills the *ever;* and there is nothing
that really is but he alone—nor can we say "He has
been," or "He will be"—without beginning and without end.

To this most religious conclusion of a pagan I want
to add only this remark of a witness of the same

condition, [14] for an ending to this long and boring 800
discourse, which would give me material without end:
"O what a vile and abject thing is man," he says,
"if he does not raise himself above humanity!"

    ᶜThat is a good statement and a useful desire, but
equally absurd. For ᴬto make the handful bigger than
the hand, the armful bigger than the arm, and to hope
to straddle more than the reach of our legs, is impossible and unnatural. Nor can man raise himself above
himself and humanity; for he can see only with his
own eyes, and seize only with his own grasp.   810

He will rise, if God by exception lends him a hand;
he will rise by abandoning and renouncing his own
means, and letting himself be raised and uplifted by
purely celestial means.

    ᶜIt is for our Christian faith, not for his Stoical
virtue, to aspire to that divine and miraculous meta-
morphosis. [15]

14. Seneca.
15. This conclusion (all that follows "raise himself above humanity!") replaced the following one, which appeared in all the
editions published during Montaigne's lifetime: "There is no truer
saying in all his Stoic school than that one. But to make the handful
bigger than the hand, the armful bigger than the arm, and to hope
to straddle more than the reach of our legs, is impossible and
unnatural. Nor can man raise himself above himself and humanity;
for he can see only with his own eyes, and seize only with his
own grasp. He will rise, if God lends him his hand; he will rise
by abandoning and renouncing his own means, and letting himself
be raised and uplifted by divine grace; but not otherwise."

BOOK III

Of Repentance[1]

[B] Others form man; I tell of him, and portray a particular one, very ill-formed, whom I should really make very different from what he is if I had to fashion him over again. But now it is done.

Now the lines of my painting do not go astray, though they change and vary. The world is but a perennial movement. All things in it are in constant motion—the earth, the rocks of the Caucasus, the pyramids of Egypt—both with the common motion and with their own. Stability itself is nothing but a more languid motion. 10

I cannot keep my subject still. It goes along befuddled and staggering, with a natural drunkenness. I take it in this condition, just as it is at the moment I give my attention to it. I do not portray being: I portray passing. Not the passing from one age to another, or, as the people say, from seven years to seven years, but from day to day, from minute to minute. My history needs to be adapted to the moment. I may presently change, not only by chance, but also by 20 intention. This is a record of various and changeable occurrences, and of irresolute and, when it so befalls, contradictory ideas: whether I am different myself, or whether I take hold of my subjects in different circumstances and aspects. So, all in all, I may indeed contradict myself now and then; but truth, as Demades said, I do not contradict. If my mind could gain a firm footing, I would not make essays, I would make decisions; but it is always in apprenticeship and on trial. 30

I set forth a humble and inglorious life; that does not matter. You can tie up all moral philosophy with a common and private life just as well as with a life

1. Chapter 2.

75

of richer stuff. Each man bears the entire form of
man's estate.

   ^{C}Authors communicate with the people by some
special extrinsic mark; I am the first to do so by
my entire being, as Michel de Montaigne, not as a
grammarian or a poet or a jurist. If the world complains
40 that I speak too much of myself, I complain that
it does not even think of itself.

   ^{B}But is it reasonable that I, so fond of privacy
in actual life, should aspire to publicity in the knowledge of me? Is it reasonable too that I should set
forth to the world, where fashioning and art have
so much credit and authority, some crude and simple
products of nature, and of a very feeble nature at
that? Is it not making a wall without stone, or something
like that, to construct books without knowledge and
50 without art? Musical fancies are guided by art, mine
by chance.

   At least I have one thing according to the rules:
that no man ever treated a subject he knew and
understood better than I do the subject I have undertaken; and that in this I am the most learned man
alive. Secondly, that no man ever ^{C}penetrated more
deeply into his material, or plucked its limbs and
consequences cleaner, or ^{B}reached more accurately
and fully the goal he had set for his work. To
60 accomplish it, I need only bring it to fidelity; and
that is in it, as sincere and pure as can be found.
I speak the truth, not my fill of it, but as much as
I dare speak; and I dare to do so a little more as
I grow old, for it seems that custom allows old age
more freedom to prate and more indiscretion in talking
about oneself. It cannot happen here as I see it
happening often, that the craftsman and his work
contradict each other: "Has a man whose conversation
is so good written such a stupid book?" or "Have
70 such learned writings come from a man whose conversation is so feeble?"

   ^{C}If a man is commonplace in conversation and rare

in writing, that means that his capacity is in the place from which he borrows it, and not in himself. A learned man is not learned in all matters; but the capable man is capable in all matters, even in ignorance.

[B] In this case we go hand in hand and at the same pace, my book and I. In other cases one may commend or blame the work apart from the workman; not so here; he who touches the one, touches the other. He 80 who judges it without knowing it will injure himself more than me; he who has known it will completely satisfy me. Happy beyond my deserts if I have just this share of public approval, that I make men of understanding feel that I was capable of profiting by knowledge, if I had had any, and that I deserved better assistance from my memory.

Let me here excuse what I often say, that I rarely repent [C] and that my conscience is content with it-self—not as the conscience of an angel or a horse, 90 but as the conscience of a man; [B] always adding this refrain, not perfunctorily but in sincere and complete submission: that I speak as an ignorant inquirer, referring the decision purely and simply to the common and authorized beliefs. I do not teach, I tell.

There is no vice truly a vice which is not offensive, and which a sound judgment does not condemn; for its ugliness and painfulness is so apparent that perhaps the people are right who say it is chiefly produced by stupidity and ignorance. So hard it is to imagine 100 anyone knowing it without hating it.

[C] Malice sucks up the greater part of its own venom, and poisons itself with it. [B] Vice leaves repentance in the soul, like an ulcer in the flesh, which is always scratching itself and drawing blood. For reason effaces other griefs and sorrows; but it engenders that of repentance, which is all the more grievous because it springs from within, as the cold and heat of fevers is sharper than that which comes from outside. I consider as vices (but each one according to its 110 measure) not only those that reason and nature condemn, but also those that man's opinion has created, even false and erroneous opinion, if it is authorized by laws and customs.

There is likewise no good deed that does not rejoice a wellborn nature. Indeed there is a sort of gratification in doing good which makes us rejoice in ourselves, and a generous pride that accompanies a good conscience. A boldly vicious soul may perhaps arm itself
120 with security, but with this complacency and satisfaction it cannot provide itself. It is no slight pleasure to feel oneself preserved from the contagion of so depraved an age, and to say to oneself: "If anyone should see right into my soul, still he would not find me guilty either of anyone's affliction or ruin, or of vengeance or envy, or of public offense against the laws, or of innovation and disturbance, or of failing in my word; and in spite of what the license of the times allows and teaches each man, still I have not
130 put my hand either upon the property or into the purse of any Frenchman, and have lived only on my own, both in war and in peace; nor have I used any man's work without paying his wages." These testimonies of conscience give us pleasure; and this natural rejoicing is a great boon to us, and the only payment that never fails us.

To found the reward for virtuous actions on the approval of others is to choose too uncertain and shaky a foundation. ^CEspecially in an age as corrupt
140 and ignorant as this, the good opinion of the people is a dishonor. Whom can you trust to see what is praiseworthy? God keep me from being a worthy man according to the descriptions I see people every day giving of themselves in their own honor. *What were vices now are moral acts* [Seneca].

Certain of my friends have sometimes undertaken to call me on the carpet and lecture me unreservedly, either of their own accord or at my invitation, as a service which, to a well-formed soul, surpasses all
150 the services of friendship, not only in usefulness, but also in pleasantness. I have always welcomed it with

the wide-open arms of courtesy and gratitude. But to speak of it now in all conscience, I have often found in their reproach or praise such false measure that I would hardly have erred to err rather than to do good in their fashion.

^BThose of us especially who live a private life that is on display only to ourselves must have a pattern established within us by which to test our actions, and, according to this pattern, now pat ourselves on 160 the back, now punish ourselves. I have my own laws and court to judge me, and I address myself to them more than anywhere else. To be sure, I restrain my actions according to others, but I extend them only according to myself. There is no one but yourself who knows whether you are cowardly and cruel, or loyal and devout. Others do not see you, they guess at you by uncertain conjectures; they see not so much your nature as your art. Therefore do not cling to their judgment; cling to your own. ^C*You must use* 170 *your own judgment. . . . With regard to virtues and vices, your own conscience has great weight: take that away, and everything falls* [Cicero].

^BBut the saying that repentance follows close upon sin does not seem to consider the sin that is in robes of state, that dwells in us as in its own home. We can disown and retract the vices that take us by surprise, and toward which we are swept by passion; but those which by long habit are rooted and anchored in a strong and vigorous will cannot be denied. Repen- 180 tance is nothing but a disavowal of our will and an opposition to our fancies, which leads us about in all directions. It makes this man disown his past virtue and his continence:

Why had I not in youth the mind I have today?
Or why, with old desires, have red cheeks flown away?

HORACE

It is a rare life that remains well ordered even in private. Any man can play his part in the side show and represent a worthy man on the boards; but to 190 be disciplined within, in his own bosom, where all is permissible, where all is concealed—that's the point. The next step to that is to be so in our own house, in our ordinary actions, for which we need render account to no one, where nothing is studied or artificial. And therefore Bias, depicting an excellent state of family life, says it is one in which the master is the same within, by his own volition, as he is outside for fear of the law and of what people will say. And

200 it was a worthy remark of Julius Drusus to the workmen who offered, for three thousand crowns, to arrange his house so that his neighbors would no longer be able to look into it as they could before. "I will give you six thousand," he said; "make it so that everyone can see in from all sides." The practice of Agesilaus is noted with honor, of taking lodging in the churches when traveling, so that people and the gods themselves might see into his private actions. Men have seemed miraculous to the world,

210 in whom their wives and valets have never seen anything even worth noticing. Few men have been admired by their own households.

°No man has been a prophet, not merely in his own house, but in his own country, says the experience of history. Likewise in things of no importance. And in this humble example you may see an image of greater ones. In my region of Gascony they think it a joke to see me in print. The farther from my lair the knowledge of me spreads, the more I am

220 valued. I buy printers in Guienne, elsewhere they buy me. On this phenomenon those people base their hopes who hide themselves while alive and present, to gain favor when dead and gone. I would rather have less of it. And I cast myself on the world only for the share of favor I get now. When I leave it, I shall hold it quits.

ᴮThe people escort this man back to his door, with awe, from a public function. He drops his part with his gown; the higher he has hoisted himself, the lower

230 he falls back; inside, in his home, everything is

tumultuous and vile. Even if there is order there,
it takes a keen and select judgment to perceive it
in these humble private actions. Besides, order is a
dull and somber virtue. To win through a breach,
to conduct an embassy, to govern a people, these
are dazzling actions. To scold, to laugh, to sell, to
pay, to love, to hate, and to deal pleasantly and justly
with our household and ourselves, not to let ourselves
go, not to be false to ourselves, that is a rarer matter,
more difficult and less noticeable.   240

Therefore retired lives, whatever people may say,
accomplish duties as harsh and strenuous as other
lives, or more so. ^CAnd private persons, says Aristotle,
render higher and more difficult service to virtue than
those who are in authority. ^BWe prepare ourselves
for eminent occasions more for glory than for conscience. ^CThe shortest way to attain glory would be
to do for conscience what we do for glory. ^BAnd
Alexander's virtue seems to me to represent much
less vigor in his theater than does that of Socrates 250
in his lowly and obscure activity. I can easily imagine
Socrates in Alexander's place; Alexander in that of
Socrates, I cannot. If you ask the former what he
knows how to do, he will answer, "Subdue the world";
if you ask the latter, he will say, "Lead the life of
man in conformity with its natural condition"; a
knowledge much more general, more weighty, and
more legitimate.

The value of the soul consists not in flying high,
but in an orderly pace. ^CIts greatness is exercised 260
not in greatness, but in mediocrity. As those who
judge and touch us inwardly make little account of
the brilliance of our public acts, and see that these
are only thin streams and jets of water spurting from
a bottom otherwise muddy and thick; so likewise those
who judge us by this brave outward appearance draw
similar conclusions about our inner constitution, and
cannot associate common faculties, just like their own,
with these other faculties that astonish them and are
so far beyond their scope. So we give demons wild 270

shapes. And who does not give Tamerlane raised eyebrows, open nostrils, a dreadful face, and immense size, like the size of the imaginary picture of him we have formed from the renown of his name? If I had been able to see Erasmus in other days, it would have been hard for me not to take for adages and apothegms everything he said to his valet and his hostess. We imagine much more appropriately an artisan on the toilet seat or on his wife than a great
280 president, venerable by his demeanor and his ability. It seems to us that they do not stoop from their lofty thrones even to live.

   [B]As vicious souls are often incited to do good by some extraneous impulse, so are virtuous souls to do evil. Thus we must judge them by their settled state, when they are at home, if ever they are; or at least when they are closest to repose and their natural position.

   Natural inclinations gain assistance and strength
290 from education; but they are scarcely to be changed and overcome. A thousand natures, in my time, have escaped toward virtue or toward vice through the lines of a contrary training:

> As when wild beasts grow tame, shut in a cage,
> Forget the woods, and lose their look of rage,
> And learn to suffer man; but if they taste
> Hot blood, their rage and fury is replaced,
> Their reminiscent jaws distend, they burn,
> And for their trembling keeper's blood they yearn.

300   LUCAN

We do not root out these original qualities, we cover them up, we conceal them. Latin is like a native tongue to me; I understand it better than French; but for forty years I have not used it at all for speaking or writing. Yet in sudden and extreme emotions, into which I have fallen two or three times in my life—one of them when I saw my father, in perfect health, fall back into my arms in a faint—I have always poured out my first words from the depths of my entrails

in Latin; ^CNature surging forth and expressing herself 310
by force, in the face of long habit. ^BAnd this experience
is told of many others.

Those who in my time have tried to correct the
world's morals by new ideas, reform the superficial
vices; the essential ones they leave as they were,
if they do not increase them; and increase is to be
feared. People are likely to rest from all other well-
doing on the strength of these external, arbitrary
reforms, which cost us less and bring greater acclaim;
and thereby they satisfy at little expense the other 320
natural, consubstantial, and internal vices.

Just consider the evidence of this in our own
experience. There is no one who, if he listens to
himself, does not discover in himself a pattern all
his own, a ruling pattern, which struggles against
education and against the tempest of the passions that
oppose it. For my part, I do not feel much sudden
agitation; I am nearly always in place, like heavy and
inert bodies. If I am not at home, I am always very
near it. My excesses do not carry me very far away. 330
There is nothing extreme or strange about them. And
besides I have periods of vigorous and healthy reac-
tion.

The real condemnation, which applies to the common run of men of today, is that even their retirement
is full of corruption and filth; their idea of reformation,
blurred; their penitence, diseased and guilty, almost
as much as their sin. Some, either from being glued
to vice by a natural attachment, or from long habit,
no longer recognize its ugliness. On others (in whose 340
regiment I belong) vice weighs heavily, but they
counterbalance it with pleasure or some other consideration, and endure it and lend themselves to it for
a certain price; viciously, however, and basely. Yet
it might be possible to imagine a disproportion so
extreme that the pleasure might justly excuse the sin,
as we say utility does; not only if the pleasure was
incidental and not a part of the sin, as in theft, but
if it was in the very exercise of the sin, as in intercourse

350 with women, where the impulse is violent, and, they
     say, sometimes invincible.
         The other day when I was at Armagnac, on the
     estate of a kinsman of mine, I saw a country fellow
     whom everyone nicknames the Thief. He gave this
     account of his life: that born a beggar, and finding
     that by earning his bread by the toil of his hands
     he would never protect himself enough against want,
     he had decided to become a thief; and he had spent
     all his youth at this trade in security, by virtue of
360 his bodily strength. For he reaped his harvest and
     vintage from other people's lands, but so far away
     and in such great loads that it was inconceivable that
     one man could have carried off so much on his
     shoulders in one night. And he was careful besides
     to equalize and spread out the damage he did, so
     that the loss was less insupportable for each individual.
     He is now, in his old age, rich for a man in his station,
     thanks to this traffic, which he openly confesses. And
     to make his peace with God for his acquisitions, he
370 says that he spends his days compensating, by good
     deeds, the successors of the people he robbed; and
     that if he does not finish this task (for he cannot
     do it all at once), he will charge his heirs with it,
     according to the knowledge, which he alone has, of
     the amount of wrong he did to each. Judging by this
     description, whether it is true or false, this man regards
     theft as a dishonorable action and hates it, but hates
     it less than poverty; he indeed repents of it in itself,
     but in so far as it was thus counterbalanced and
380 compensated, he does not repent of it. This is not
     that habit that incorporates us with vice and brings
     even our understanding into conformity with it; nor
     is it that impetuous wind that comes in gusts to confuse
     and blind our soul, and hurls us for the moment
     headlong, judgment and all, into the power of vice.
         I customarily do wholeheartedly whatever I do, and
     go my way all in one piece. I scarcely make a motion
     that is hidden and out of sight of my reason, and
     that is not guided by the consent of nearly all parts

of me, without division, without internal sedition. My 390
judgment takes all the blame or all the praise for
it; and the blame it once takes, it always keeps, for
virtually since its birth it has been one; the same
inclination, the same road, the same strength. And
in the manner of general opinions, in childhood I
established myself in the position where I was to
remain.

There are some impetuous, prompt, and sudden sins:
let us leave them aside. But as for these other sins
so many times repeated, planned, and premeditated, 400
constitutional sins, ^Cor even professional or vocational
sins, ^BI cannot imagine that they can be implanted
so long in one and the same heart, without the reason
and conscience of their possessor constantly willing
and intending it to be so. And the repentance which
he claims comes to him at a certain prescribed moment
is a little hard for me to imagine and conceive.

^CI do not follow the belief of the sect of Pythagoras,
that men take on a new soul when they approach
the images of the gods to receive their oracles. Unless 410
he meant just this, that the soul must indeed be foreign,
new, and loaned for the occasion, since their own
showed so little sign of any purification and cleanness
worthy of this office.

^BThey do just the opposite of the Stoic precepts,
which indeed order us to correct the imperfections
and vices that we recognize in us, but forbid us to
be repentant and glum about them. These men make
us believe that they feel great regret and remorse
within; but of amendment and correction, ^Cor inter- 420
ruption, ^Bthey show us no sign. Yet it is no cure
if the disease is not thrown off. If repentance were
weighing in the scale of the balance, it would outweigh
the sin. I know of no quality so easy to counterfeit
as piety, if conduct and life are not made to conform
with it. Its essence is abstruse and occult; its semblance, easy and showy.

As for me, I may desire in a general way to be
different; I may condemn and dislike my nature as

430 a whole, and implore God to reform me completely and to pardon my natural weakness. But this I ought not to call repentance, it seems to me, any more than my displeasure at being neither an angel nor Cato. My actions are in order and conformity with what I am and with my condition. I can do no better. And repentance does not properly apply to the things that are not in our power; rather does regret. I imagine numberless natures loftier and better regulated than mine, but for all that, I do not amend my faculties;

440 just as neither my arm nor my mind becomes more vigorous by imagining another that is so. If imagining and desiring a nobler conduct than ours produced repentance of our own, we should have to repent of our most innocent actions, inasmuch as we rightly judge that in a more excellent nature they would have been performed with greater perfection and dignity, and we should wish to do likewise.

When I consider the behavior of my youth in comparison with that of my old age, I find that I

450 have generally conducted myself in orderly fashion, according to my lights; that is all my resistance can accomplish. I do not flatter myself; in similar circumstances I should always be the same. It is not a spot, it is rather a tincture with which I am stained all over. I know no superficial, halfway, and perfunctory repentance. It must affect me in every part before I will call it so, and must grip me by the vitals and afflict them as deeply and as completely as God sees into me.

460 In business matters, several good opportunities have escaped me for want of successful management. However, my counsels have been good, according to the circumstances they were faced with; their way is always to take the easiest and surest course. I find that in my past deliberations, according to my rule, I have proceeded wisely, considering the state of the matter proposed to me, and I should do the same a thousand years from now in similar situations. I am not considering what it is at this moment, but

what it was when I was deliberating about it. 470
^CThe soundness of any plan depends on the time; circumstances and things roll about and change incessantly. I have fallen into some serious and important mistakes in my life, not for lack of good counsel but for lack of good luck. There are secret parts in the matters we handle which cannot be guessed, especially in human nature—mute factors that do not show, factors sometimes unknown to their possessor himself, which are brought forth and aroused by unexpected occasions. If my prudence has been unable 480 to see into them and predict them, I bear it no ill will; its responsibility is restricted within its limitations. It is the outcome that beats me; and ^Bif it favors the course I have refused, there is no help for it; I do not blame myself; I accuse my luck, not my work. That is not to be called repentance.

Phocion had given the Athenians some advice that was not followed. When however the affair came out prosperously against his opinion, someone said to him: "Well, Phocion, are you glad that the thing is going 490 so well?" "Indeed I am glad," he said, "that it has turned out this way, but I do not repent of having advised that way."

When my friends apply to me for advice, I give it freely and clearly, and without hesitating as nearly everyone else does because, the affair being hazardous, it may come out contrary to my expectations, wherefore they may have cause to reproach me for my advice; that does not worry me. For they will be wrong, and I should not have refused them this 500 service.

^CI have scarcely any occasion to blame my mistakes or mishaps on anyone but myself. For in practice I rarely ask other people's advice, unless as a compliment and out of politeness, except when I need scientific information or knowledge of the facts. But in things where I have only my judgment to employ, other people's reasons can serve to support me, but seldom to change my course. I listen to them all

510 favorably and decently; but so far as I can remember,
I have never up to this moment followed any but
my own. If you ask me, they are nothing but flies
and atoms that distract my will. I set little value on
my own opinions, but I set just as little on those
of others. Fortune pays me properly. If I do not take
advice, I give still less. Mine is seldom asked, but
it is followed even less; and I know of no public
or private enterprise that my advice restored to its
feet and to the right path. Even the people whom
520 fortune has made somewhat dependent on it have
let themselves be managed more readily by anyone
else's brains. Being a man who is quite as jealous
of the rights of my repose as of the rights of my
authority, I prefer it so; by leaving me alone, they
treat me according to my professed principle, which
is to be wholly contained and established within
myself. To me it is a pleasure not to be concerned
in other people's affairs and to be free of responsibility
for them.
530   B In all affairs, when they are past, however they
have turned out, I have little regret. For this idea
takes away the pain: that they were bound to happen
thus, and now they are in the great stream of the
universe and in the chain of Stoical causes. Your
fancy, by wish or imagination, cannot change a single
point without overturning the whole order of things,
and the past and the future.

For the rest, I hate that accidental repentance that
age brings. The man who said of old that he was
540 obliged to the years for having rid him of sensuality
had a different viewpoint from mine; I shall never
be grateful to impotence for any good it may do me.
C Nor will Providence ever be so hostile to her own
work that debility should be ranked among the best
things [Quintilian]. B Our appetites are few in old age;
a profound satiety seizes us after the act. In that
I see nothing of conscience; sourness and weakness
imprint on us a sluggish and rheumatic virtue. We
must not let ourselves be so carried away by natural

changes as to let our judgment degenerate. Youth 550
and pleasure in other days did not make me fail to
recognize the face of vice in voluptuousness; nor does
the distaste that the years bring me make me fail
to recognize the face of voluptuousness in vice. Now
that I am no longer in that state, I judge it as though
I were in it.

   ᶜI who shake up my reason sharply and attentively,
find that ᴮit is the very same I had in my more licentious
years, except perhaps in so far as it has grown weaker
and worse as it has grown old. ᶜAnd I find that even 560
if it refuses, out of consideration for the interests
of my bodily health, to put me in the furnace of this
pleasure, it would not refuse to do so, any more than
formerly, for my spiritual health. ᴮI do not consider
it any more valiant for seeing it *hors de combat*. My
temptations are so broken and mortified that they
are not worth its opposition. By merely stretching
out my hands to them, I exorcise them. If my reason
were confronted with my former lust, I fear that it
would have less strength to resist than it used to have. 570
I do not see that of itself it judges anything differently
than it did then, nor that it has gained any new light.
Wherefore, if there is any convalescence, it is a deformed convalescence.

   ᶜMiserable sort of remedy, to owe our health to
disease! It is not for our misfortune to do us this
service, it is for the good fortune of our judgment.
You cannot make me do anything by ills and afflictions
except curse them. They are for people who are only
awakened by whipping. My reason runs a much freer 580
course in prosperity. It is much more distracted and
busy digesting pains than pleasures. I see much more
clearly in fair weather. Health admonishes me more
cheerfully and so more usefully than sickness. I
advanced as far as I could toward reform and a
regulated life when I had health to enjoy. I should
be ashamed and resentful if the misery and misfortune
of my decrepitude were to be thought better than
my good, healthy, lively, vigorous years, and if people

590 were to esteem me not for what I have been, but for ceasing to be that.

In my opinion it is living happily, not, as Antisthenes said, dying happily, that constitutes human felicity. I have made no effort to attach, monstrously, the tail of a philosopher to the head and body of a dissipated man; or that this sickly remainder of my life should disavow and belie its fairest, longest, and most complete part. I want to present and show myself uniformly throughout. If I had to live over again, 600 I would live as I have lived. I have neither tears for the past nor fears for the future. And unless I am fooling myself, it has gone about the same way within me as without. It is one of the chief obligations I have to my fortune that my bodily state has run its course with each thing in due season. I have seen the grass, the flower, and the fruit; now I see the dryness—happily, since it is naturally. I bear the ills I have much more easily because they are properly timed, and also because they make me remember more 610 pleasantly the long felicity of my past life.

Likewise my wisdom may well have been of the same proportions in one age as in the other; but it was much more potent and graceful when green, gay, and natural, than it is now, being broken down, peevish, and labored. Therefore I renounce these casual and painful reformations.

[B]God must touch our hearts. Our conscience must reform by itself through the strengthening of our reason, not through the weakening of our appetites. 620 Sensual pleasure is neither pale nor colorless in itself for being seen through dim and bleary eyes. We should love temperance for itself and out of reverence toward God, who has commanded it, and also chastity; what catarrh lends us, and what I owe to the favor of my colic, is neither chastity nor temperance. We cannot boast of despising and fighting sensual pleasure, if we do not see or know it, and its charms, its powers, and its most alluring beauty.

I know them both; I have a right to speak; but

it seems to me that in old age our souls are subject 630
to more troublesome ailments and imperfections than
in our youth. I used to say so when I was young;
then they taunted me with my beardless chin. I still
say so now that my ^Cgray ^Bhair gives me authority
to speak. We call "wisdom" the difficulty of our
humors, our distaste for present things. But in truth
we do not so much abandon our vices as change them,
and, in my opinion, for the worse. Besides a silly
and decrepit pride, a 'tedious prattle, prickly and
unsociable humors, superstition, and a ridiculous con- 640
cern for riches when we have lost the use of them,
I find there more envy, injustice, and malice. Old
age puts more wrinkles in our minds than on our
faces; and we never, or rarely, see a soul that in
growing old does not come to smell sour and musty.
Man grows and dwindles in his entirety.

   ^CSeeing the wisdom of Socrates and several circumstances of his condemnation, I should venture to
believe that he lent himself to it to some extent,
purposely, by prevarication, being seventy, and having 650
so soon to suffer an increasing torpor of the rich
activity of his mind, and the dimming of its accustomed
brightness.

   ^BWhat metamorphoses I see old age producing every
day in many of my acquaintances! It is a powerful
malady, and it creeps up on us naturally and impercep-
tibly. We need a great provision of study, and great
precaution, to avoid the imperfections it loads upon
us, or at least to slow up their progress. I feel that,
notwithstanding all my retrenchments, it gains on me 660
foot by foot. I stand fast as well as I can. But I
do not know where it will lead even me in the end.
In any event, I am glad to have people know whence
I shall have fallen.

Of Husbanding
Your Will [1]

[B] In comparison with most men, few things touch me, or, to put it better, hold me; for it is right that things should touch us, provided they do not possess us. I take great care to augment by study and reasoning this privilege of insensibility, which is naturally well advanced in me. I espouse, and in consequence grow passionate about, few things. My sight is clear, but I fix it on few objects; my sensitivity is delicate and tender. But my perception and application are hard
10 and deaf: I do not engage myself easily. As much as I can, I employ myself entirely upon myself; and even in that subject I would still fain bridle my affection and keep it from plunging in too entirely, since this is a subject that I possess at the mercy of others, and over which fortune has more right than I have. So that even in regard to health, which I so esteem, I ought not to desire it and give myself to it so frantically as to find illnesses therefore unbearable. [C] One must moderate oneself between hatred of pain
20 and love of pleasure; and Plato prescribes a middle way of life between the two.

[B] But the passions that distract me from myself and attach me elsewhere, those in truth I oppose with all my strength. My opinion is that we must lend ourselves to others and give ourselves only to ourselves. If my will happened to be prone to mortgage and attach itself, I would not last: I am too tender, both by nature and by practice,

Fleeing affairs, and born in idle ease.

30   OVID

1. Chapter 10.

92

To engage in contested disputes only to see my
opponent get the better of me, or to have to turn
back red-faced after giving hot pursuit, might well
vex me cruelly. If I were to bite off as much as
others do, my soul would never have the strength
to bear the alarms and emotions that afflict those
who embrace so much; it would be put out of joint
from the start by this inner agitation.

If people have sometimes pushed me into the management of other men's affairs, I have promised to   40
take them in hand, not in lungs and liver; to take
them on my shoulders, not incorporate them into me;
to be concerned over them, yes; to be impassioned
over them, never. I look to them, but I do not brood
over them. I have enough to do to order and arrange
the domestic pressures that oppress my entrails and
veins, without giving myself the trouble of adding
extraneous pressures to them; I am enough involved
in my essential, proper, and natural affairs, without
inviting in foreign ones.   50

Those who know how much they owe to themselves,
and for how many duties they are obligated to themselves, find that nature has given them in this a
commission full enough and not at all idle. You have
quite enough to do at home; don't go away.

Men give themselves for hire. Their faculties are
not for them, they are for those to whom they enslave
themselves; their tenants are at home inside, not they.
This common humor I do not like. We must husband
the freedom of our soul and mortgage it only on the   60
right occasions; which are in very small number, if
we judge sanely. See the people who have been taught
to let themselves be seized and carried away: they
do so everywhere, in little things as in big, in what
does not touch them as in what does; they push in
indiscriminately wherever there is business ^cand in-
volvement, ^B and are without life when they are without
tumultuous agitation. ^C *They are in business for business' sake* [Seneca]. They seek business only for
busyness.   70

It is not that they want to be on the go, so much as that they cannot keep still; no more nor less than a stone that has started falling, and that does not stop until it comes to rest. Occupation is to a certain manner of people a mark of ability and dignity. ^BTheir mind seeks its repose in movement, like children in the cradle. They may be said to be as serviceable to their friends as they are importunate to themselves. No one distributes his money to others, everyone

80 distributes his time and his life on them. There is nothing of which we are so prodigal as of the only things in which avarice would be useful to us and laudable.

I take a wholly different attitude. I keep myself to myself, and commonly desire mildly what I desire, and desire little; occupy and busy myself likewise; rarely and tranquilly. Whatever they desire and take in hand, they do with all their will and vehemence. There are so many bad spots that, for greatest safety,

90 we must slide over this world a bit lightly and on the surface. ^CWe must glide over it, not break through into it. ^BEven sensual pleasure is painful in its depth:

> Treacherous ashes hide
> The fires through which you stride.
>
> HORACE

Messieurs of Bordeaux[2] elected me mayor of their city when I was far from France and still farther from such a thought. I excused myself, but I was informed that I was wrong, since the king's command

100 also figured in the matter. It is an office that must appear all the handsomer for this, that it has no remuneration or gain other than the honor of its execution. The term is two years; but it can be extended by a second election, which happens very rarely. This was done in my case, and had been done only twice before: some years earlier to Monsieur de Lansac,

2. The jurats, who formed a sort of municipal council.

and recently to Monsieur de Biron, Marshal of France, to whose place I succeeded; and I left mine to Monsieur de Matignon, also Marshal of France, proud of such noble company,   110

^CEach a good minister in peace and war.

VIRGIL.

^BFortune willed to have a hand in my promotion by this particular circumstance that she put in of her own. Not wholly vain: for Alexander disdained the Corinthian ambassadors who were offering him citizenship in their city; but when they came to tell him that Bacchus and Hercules were also on that list, he thanked them graciously for their offer.

On my arrival I deciphered myself to them faithfully 120 and conscientiously, exactly such as I feel myself to be: without memory, without vigilance, without experience, and without vigor; also without hate, without ambition, without avarice, and without violence; so that they should be informed and instructed about what they were to expect of my service. And because their knowledge of my late father had alone incited them to this, and their honor for his memory,[3] I added very clearly that I should be very sorry if anything whatsoever were to weigh so heavily on my 130 will as their affairs and their city had formerly done on his, while he was administering it in this same spot to which they had called me.

I remembered in my boyhood having seen him old, his soul cruelly agitated by this public turmoil, forgetting the sweet air of his home, to which the weakness of years had attached him long since, and his household and his health; and, truly heedless of his life, which he nearly lost in this, engaged for them in long and

.3. Probably Montaigne sincerely believed this; but it now seems more likely that he was elected because he was the man most acceptable to all four royal personages concerned with the election: Henry III, Catherine de' Medici, Henry of Navarre, and Margaret of Valois. See Alexandre Nicolaï, *Les Belles Amies de Montaigne* (1950), pp. 135-45.

140 painful journeys. He was like that; and this disposition
in him sprang from a great goodness of nature: there
was never a more kindly and public-spirited soul.

This course, which I commend in others, I do not
love to follow, and I am not without excuse. He had
heard it said that we must forget ourselves for our
neighbor, that the individual was not to be considered
at all in comparison with the general.

Most of the rules and precepts of the world take
this course of pushing us out of ourselves and driving
150 us into the market place, for the benefit of public
society. They thought to achieve a fine result by
diverting and distracting us from ourselves, assuming
that we were attached to ourselves only too much
and by too natural a bond; and they have spared no
words to that end. For it is not new for the sages
to preach things as they serve, not as they are. ^CTruth
has its inconveniences, disadvantages, and incompat-
ibilities with us. We must often be deceived that we
may not deceive ourselves, and our eyes sealed, our
160 understanding stunned, in order to redress and amend
them. *For it is the ignorant who judge, and they must
frequently be deceived, lest they err* [Quintilian].
^BWhen they order us to love three, four, fifty degrees
of things before ourselves, they imitate the technique
of the archers who, to hit the mark, take aim a great
distance above the target. To straighten a bent stick
you bend it back the other way.

I think that in the temple of Pallas, as we see in
all other religions, there were apparent mysteries to
170 be shown to the people, and other mysteries, more
secret and high, to be shown only to those who were
initiated. It is likely that among the latter is to be
found the true point of the friendship that each man
owes to himself. Not ^Ca false friendship, that makes
us embrace glory, learning, riches,. and such things
with paramount and immoderate affection, as members
of our being; nor ^Ban overindulgent and undiscrimi-
nating friendship, in which it happens as we see with
ivy, that it decays and ruins the wall it clings to;

but a salutary and well-regulated friendship, useful 180
and pleasant alike. He who knows its duties and
practices them, he is truly of the cabinet of the Muses;
he has attained the summit of human wisdom and
of our happiness. This man, knowing exactly what
he owes to himself, finds it in his part that he is
to apply to himself his experience of other men and
of the world, and, in order to do so, contribute to
public society the duties and services within his prov-
ince. ^CHe who lives not at all unto others, hardly
lives unto himself. *He who is a friend to himself,* 190
know that that man is a friend to all [Seneca].

^BThe main responsibility of each of us is his own
conduct; ^Cand that is what we are here for. ^BJust
as anyone who should forget to live a good and saintly
life, and think he was quit of his duty by guiding
and training others to do so, would be a fool; even
so he who abandons healthy and gay living of his
own to serve others thereby, takes, to my taste, a
bad and unnatural course.

I do not want a man to refuse, to the charges he 200
takes on, attention, steps, words, and sweat and blood
if need be:

> To die for what is dear,
> Country or friends, I do not fear.
>
> HORACE

But this is by way of loan and accidentally, the mind
holding itself ever in repose and in health, not without
action, but without vexation, without passion. Simply
to act costs it so little that it is acting even in sleep.
But it must be set in motion with discretion. For the 210
body receives the loads that are placed on it exactly
according as they are; the mind often extends them
and makes them heavier to its cost, giving them the
measurements it sees fit. We do like things with
different degrees of effort and tension of the will.
The one goes very well without the other.[4] For how

4. Action without passion.

many people risk themselves every day in the wars, which are no concern to them, and press forward to the dángers of battles, the loss of which will not
220 trouble their next night's sleep! This man in his own house, outside of this danger which he would not have dared to face, is more passionate about the outcome of this war, and more worked up in his soul about it, than the soldier who is spending his blood and his life in it.

I have been able to take part in public office without departing one nail's breadth from myself, ^Cand to give myself to others without taking myself from myself. ^BThis fierceness and violence of desire hinders
230 more than it serves the performance of what we undertake, fills us with impatience toward things that come out contrary or late, and with bitterness and suspicion toward the people we deal with. We never conduct well the thing that possesses and conducts us....

Most of our occupations are low comedy. *The whole world plays a part* [Petronius]. We must play our part duly, but as the part of a borrowed character. Of the mask and appearance we must not make a
240 real essence, nor of what is foreign what is our very own. We cannot distinguish the skin from the shirt. ^CIt is enough to make up our face, without making up our heart. ^BI see some who transform and transubstantiate themselves into as many new shapes and new beings as they undertake jobs, who are prelates to their very liver and intestines, and drag their position with them even into their privy. I cannot teach them to distinguish the the tips of the hat that are for them from those that are for their office, or their retinue,
250 or their mule. *They give themselves up so much to their fortune that they even unlearn their natures* [Quintus Curtius]. They swell and inflate their soul and their natural speech to the height of their magisterial seat.

The mayor and Montaigne have always been two, with a very clear separation. For all of being a lawyer

.

or a financier, we must not ignore the knavery there
is in such callings. An honest man is not accountable
for the vice or stupidity of his trade, and should not
therefore refuse to practice it: it is the custom of 260
his country, and there is profit in it. We must live
in the world and make the most of it such as we
find it. But the judgment of an emperor should be
above his imperial power, and see and consider it
as an extraneous accident; and he should know how
to find pleasure in himself apart, and to reveal himself
like any Jack or Peter, at least to himself....

[B] I had nothing to do but conserve and endure, which
are noiseless and imperceptible acts. Innovation has
great luster, but it is forbidden in these times, when 270
we are hard pressed and have to defend ourselves
mainly against innovations. [C] Abstention from doing
is often as noble as doing, but it is less open to the
light; and the little that I am worth is almost all on
that side.

[B] In short, the occasions in my term of office were
suited to my disposition, for which I am very grateful
to them. Is there anyone who wants to be sick in
order to see his doctor at work, and shouldn't we
whip any doctor who would wish us the plague in 280
order to put his art into practice? I have not had
that iniquitous and rather common disposition of
wanting the trouble and sickness of the affairs of
this city to exalt and honor my government; I heartily
lent a shoulder to make them easy and light. Anyone
who will not be grateful to me for the order, the
gentle and mute tranquillity, that accompanied my
administration, at least cannot deprive me of the share
of it that belongs to me by right of my good fortune.
And I am so made that I like as well to be lucky 290
as wise, and to owe my successes purely to the grace
of God as to the effect of my own action.

I had published elaborately enough to the world
my inadequacy in such public management. I have
something still worse than inadequacy: that I hardly
mind it, and hardly try to cure it, in view of the

Of Physiognomy [1]

^BI once took pleasure in seeing men in some place, through piety, take a vow of ignorance, as one might of chastity, poverty, penitence. It is also castrating our disorderly appetites, to blunt that cupidity that pricks us on to the study of books, and to deprive the soul of that voluptuous complacency which tickles us with the notion of being learned. ^CAnd it is accomplishing richly the vow of poverty to add to it also that of the mind.

^BWe need hardly any learning to live at ease. And Socrates teaches us that it is in us, and the way to find it and help ourselves with it. All this ability of ours that is beyond the natural is as good as vain and superfluous. It is a lot if it does not load us down and bother us more than it serves us. ^C*Little learning is needed for a good mind* [Seneca]. ^BThese are feverish excesses of our mind, a meddlesome and restless instrument.

Collect yourself: you will find in yourself Nature's arguments against death, true ones, and the fittest to serve you in case of necessity; they are the ones that make a peasant, and whole nations, die as steadfastly as a philosopher.

^CShould I have died less cheerfully before having read the *Tusculans*?[2] I think not. And now that I find myself close to death, I feel that my tongue has grown richer, my courage not at all. This is as Nature made it for me, and arms itself for the conflict in a common and ordinary way. Books have served me not so much for instruction as for exercise.

What if ^Bknowledge, trying to arm us with new defenses against natural mishaps, has imprinted in

1. Chapter 12.
2. Cicero's *Tusculan Disputations*, of which the first book deals with contempt of death.

our fancy their magnitude and weight, more than her reasons and subtleties to protect us from them? ^CThey are subtleties indeed, with which she often alarms us very idly. Authors, even the most compact and the wisest—around one good argument see how many others they strew, trivial ones, and if you look at them closely, bodiless. These are nothing but verbal
40   quibbles, to deceive us. But inasmuch as this may be done usefully, I do not want to expose them any further. There are enough of that sort in this book in various places, either from borrowing or from imitation. Yet we should take a little care not to call strength what is only nicety, or solid what is only acute, or good what is only beautiful: *which delight more tasted than drunk* [Cicero]. Not all that entertains us sustains us, *when it is a question not of the wit but of the soul* [Seneca].
50   ^BTo see the trouble to which Seneca puts himself to be prepared for death, to see him sweat from the exertion of steeling and reassuring himself, and writhe about interminably on his perch, would have shaken his reputation with me if he had not very valiantly maintained it in dying. His agitation, so burning, so frequent, ^Cshows that he was hot and impetuous himself. *A great soul speaks more relaxedly and assuredly. . . . There is not one color for the mind, another for the soul* [Seneca]. We have to convince
60   him at his own expense.[3] And it ^Bshows perceptibly that he was hard pressed by his adversary.
     Plutarch's manner, inasmuch as it is more disdainful and less tense, is, to my mind, all the more virile and persuasive; I would easily believe that the movements of his soul were more assured and more regulated. The one, sharper, pricks us and startles us, touches our mind more. The other, more sedate, forms us, settles and fortifies us constantly, touches our understanding more. ^CThe former ravishes our judgment,
70   the latter wins it.

     3. In other words, by his own arguments, which Montaigne has quoted.

I have likewise seen other writings, still more revered, which, in portraying the conflict their authors sustain against the goads of the flesh, show these so stinging, so powerful and invincible that we, who are of the refuse of the people, have as much to wonder at in the strangeness and unheard-of vigor of their temptation as in their resistance.

^BTo what end do we keep forcing our nature with these efforts of learning? Let us look on the earth at the poor people we see scattered there, heads bowed   80 over their toil, who know neither Aristotle nor Cato, neither example nor precept. From them Nature every day draws deeds of constancy and endurance purer and harder than those that we study with such care in school. How many of them I see all the time who ignore poverty! How many who desire death, or who meet it without alarm and without affliction! This man who is digging up my garden, this morning he buried his father or his son. The very names by which they call diseases relieve and soften their harshness: phthi-   90 sis is the cough to them; dysentery, looseness of the bowels; pleurisy, a cold; and according as they name them mildly, so also they endure them. A disease must be very grave to interrupt their ordinary work; they take to their beds only to die. ^C*That simple and open virtue has been converted into obscure and subtle knowledge* [Seneca].

^BI was writing this about the time when a mighty load of our disturbances settled down for several months with all its weight right on me. I had on the   100 one hand the enemy at my door, on the other hand the freebooters, worse enemies: ^C*they fight not with arms but with vices* [Livy]; ^Band I was sampling every kind of military mischief all at once.

To right and left appears the dreaded foe,
On either side the threat of instant woe.

OVID

Monstrous war! Other wars act outward; this one acts also against itself, eats and destroys itself by its own

110 venom. It is by nature so malignant and ruinous that
it ruins itself together with all the rest, and tears and
dismembers itself with rage. We see it more often
dissolving of itself than for lack of any necessary
thing or through the power of the enemy. All discipline
flies from it. It comes to cure sedition and is full
of it, would chastise disobedience and sets the example
of it; and employed in defense of the laws, plays
the part of a rebel against its own laws. What have
we come to? Our medicine carries infection:

120   Poison to our disease
                            Are all these remedies.

                       AUTHOR UNKNOWN

     Grows all the stronger, all the sicker, with the cure.

                                    VIRGIL

          Our mad confounding of all good and ill
          Has made the gods avert their righteous will.

                            CATULLUS

     In these epidemics one can distinguish at the begin-
ning the well from the sick; but when they come to
130 last, like ours, the whole body is affected, head and
heels alike; no part is free from corruption. For there
is no air that is inhaled so greedily, that so spreads
and penetrates, as does license. Our armies are no
longer¹ bound and held together except by foreign
cement; of Frenchmen one can no longer form a
steadfast and disciplined army corps. How shameful!
There is only so much discipline as borrowed soldiers
show us; as for ourselves, we follow our own lead
and not our leader's, every man his own way. The
140 leader has more trouble within than without. It is
for the commander to follow, court, and bend, for
him alone to obey; all the rest is free and dissolute.
It pleases me to see how much baseness and pusillanimity there is in ambition, by how much abjection
and servility it must attain its goal. But this displeases
me, to see decent natures, capable of justice, grow

corrupt every day in managing and commanding this confusion. Long sufferance begets custom, custom consent and imitation. We had enough illborn souls without spoiling the good and generous ones. So that, 150 if we keep this up, there will hardly be anyone left to whom to entrust the health of this state, in case fortune restores it to us.

Of Experience[1]

^BThere is no desire more natural than the desire for knowledge. We try all the ways that can lead us to it. When reason fails us, we use experience—

^CExperience, by example led,
By varied trials art has bred
MANILIUS

—^Bwhich is a weaker and less dignified means. But truth is so great a thing that we must not disdain any medium that will lead us to it. Reason has so
10 many shapes that we know not which to lay hold of; experience has no fewer. The inference that we try to draw from the resemblance of events is uncertain, because they are always dissimilar: there is no quality so universal in this aspect of things as diversity and variety.

Both the Greeks and the Latins, and we ourselves, use eggs for the most express example of similarity. However, there have been men, and notably one at Delphi, who recognized marks of difference between
20 eggs, so that he never took one for another; ^Cand although there were many hens, he could tell which one the egg came from.

^BDissimilarity necessarily intrudes into our works; no art can attain similarity. Neither Perrozet nor any other can smooth and whiten the backs of his cards so carefully that some gamesters will not distinguish them simply by seeing them slip through another man's hands. Resemblance does not make things so much alike as difference makes them unlike. ^CNature has
30 committed herself to make nothing separate that was not different.

^BTherefore I do not much like the opinion of the man who thought by a multiplicity of laws to bridle

1. Chapter 13.

106

the authority of judges, cutting up their meat for them. He did not realize that there is as much freedom and latitude in the interpretation of laws as in their creation. And those people must be jesting who think they can diminish and stop our disputes by recalling us to the express words of the Bible. For our mind finds the field no less spacious in registering the meaning of   40 others than in presenting its own. As if there were less animosity and bitterness in commenting than in inventing!

We see how mistaken he was. For we have in France more laws than all the rest of the world together, and more than would be needed to rule all the worlds of Epicurus: ^C*As formerly we suffered from crimes, so now we suffer from laws* [Tacitus]. ^BAnd yet we have left so much room for opinion and decision to our judges, that there never was such a powerful and   50 licentious freedom. What have our legislators gained by selecting a hundred thousand particular cases and actions, and applying a hundred thousand laws to them? This number bears no proportion to the infinite diversity of human actions. Multiplication of our imaginary cases will never equal the variety of the real examples. Add to them a hundred times as many more: and still no future event will be found to correspond so exactly to any one of all the many, many thousands of selected and recorded events that   60 there will not remain some circumstance, some difference, that will require separate consideration in forming a judgment. There is little relation between our actions, which are in perpetual mutation, and fixed and immutable laws. The most desirable laws are those that are rarest, simplest, and most general; and I even think that it would be better to have none at all than to have them in such numbers as we have.

Nature always gives us happier laws than those we give ourselves. Witness the picture of the Golden   70 Age of the poets, and the state in which we see nations live which have no other laws. Here are some who employ, as the only judge in their quarrels, the first traveler passing through their mountains. And these others on market day elect one of themselves who decides all their suits on the spot. What would be the danger in having our wisest men settle ours in this way, according to the circumstances and at sight, without being bound to precedents, past or future?

80 For every foot its own shoe. King Ferdinand, when he sent colonists to the Indies, wisely provided that no students of jurisprudence should accompany them, for fear that lawsuits might breed in this new world, this being by nature a science generating altercation and division; judging, with Plato, that lawyers and doctors are a bad provision for a country.

Why is it that our common language, so easy for any other use, becomes obscure and unintelligible in contracts and wills, and that a man who expresses

90 himself so clearly, whatever he says or writes, finds in this field no way of speaking his mind that does not fall into doubt and contradiction? Unless it is that the princes of this art, applying themselves with particular attention to picking out solemn words and contriving artificial phrases, have so weighed every syllable, so minutely examined every sort of combination, that here they are at last entangled and embroiled in the endless number of figures and in such minute partitions that they can no longer fall under any rule

100 or prescription or any certain interpretation. *ᶜWhat is broken up into dust becomes confused* [Seneca].

ᴮWho has seen children trying to divide a mass of quicksilver into a certain number of parts? The more they press it and knead it and try to constrain it to their will, the more they provoke the independence of this spirited metal; it escapes their skill and keeps dividing and scattering in little particles beyond all reckoning. This is the same; for by subdividing these subtleties they teach men to increase their doubts;

110 they start us extending and diversifying the difficulties, they lengthen them, they scatter them. By sowing questions and cutting them up, they make the world fructify and teem with uncertainty and quarrels, ᶜas

the earth is made more fertile the more it is crumbled and deeply plowed. *Learning makes difficulties* [Quintilian].

[B]We were perplexed over Ulpian, we are still perplexed over Bartolus and Baldus. We should have wiped out the traces of this innumerable diversity of opinions, instead of wearing them as decoration 120 and cramming the heads of posterity with them.

I do not know what to say about it, but it is evident from experience that so many interpretations disperse the truth and shatter it. Aristotle wrote to be understood; if he did not succeed, still less will another man, less able, and not treating his own ideas. By diluting the substance we allow it to escape and spill it all over the place; of one subject we make a thousand, and, multiplying and subdividing, fall back into Epicurus' infinity of atoms. Never did two men judge 130 alike about the same thing, and it is impossible to find two opinions exactly alike, not only in different men, but in the same man at different times. Ordinarily I find subject for doubt in what the commentary has not deigned to touch on. I am more apt to trip on flat ground, like certain horses I know which stumble more often on a smooth road.

Who would not say that glosses increase doubts and ignorance, since there is no book to be found, whether human or divine, with which the world busies 140 itself, whose difficulties are cleared up by interpretation? The hundredth commentator hands it on to his successor thornier and rougher than the first one had found it. When do we agree and say, "There has been enough about this book; henceforth there is nothing more to say about it"?

This is best seen in law practice. We give legal authority to numberless doctors, numberless decisions, and as many interpretations. Do we therefore find any end to the need of interpreting? Do we see 150 any progress and advance toward tranquillity? Do we need fewer lawyers and judges than when this mass of law was still in its infancy? On the contrary, we obscure and bury the meaning; we no longer find it except hidden by so many enclosures and barriers.

Men do not know the natural infirmity of their mind: it does nothing but ferret and quest, and keeps incessantly whirling around, building up and becoming entangled in its own work, like our silkworms, and
160 is suffocated in it. *A mouse in a pitch barrel* [Erasmus]. It thinks it notices from a distance some sort of glimmer of imaginary light and truth; but while running toward it, it is crossed by so many difficulties and obstacles, and diverted by so many new quests, that it strays from the road, bewildered. Not very different from what happened to Aesop's dogs, who, discovering something that looked like a dead body floating in the sea, and being unable to approach it, attempted to drink up the water and dry up the passage, and
170 choked in the attempt. ^CTo which may be joined what a certain Crates said of the writings of Heraclitus, that they needed a good swimmer for a reader, so that the depth and weight of Heraclitus' learning should not sink him and drown him.

^BIt is only personal weakness that makes us content with what others or we ourselves have found out in this hunt for knowledge. An abler man will not rest content with it. There is always room for a successor, ^Cyes, and for ourselves, ^Band a road in another
180 direction. There is no end to our researches; our end is in the other world. ^CIt is a sign of contraction of the mind when it is content, or of weariness. A spirited mind never stops within itself; it is always aspiring and going beyond its strength; it has impulses beyond its powers of achievement. If it does not advance and press forward and stand at bay and clash, it is only half alive. ^BIts pursuits are boundless and without form; its food is ^Cwonder, the chase, ^Bambiguity. Apollo revealed this clearly enough, always
190 speaking to us equivocally, obscurely, and obliquely, not satisfying us, but keeping our minds interested and busy. It is an irregular, perpetual motion, without

model and without aim. Its inventions excite, pursue, and produce one another.

> So in a running stream one wave we see
> After another roll incessantly,
> And line by line, each does eternally
> Pursue the other, each the other flee.
> By this one, that one ever on is sped,
> And this one by the other ever led;   200
> The water still does into water go,
> Still the same brook, but different waters flow.

LA BOÉTIE

It is more of a job to interpret the interpretations than to interpret the things, and there are more books about books than about any other subject: we do nothing but write glosses about each other. ^CThe world is swarming with commentaries; of authors there is a great scarcity.

Is it not the chief and most reputed learning of 210 our times to learn to understand the learned? Is that not the common and ultimate end of all studies?

Our opinions are grafted upon one another. The first serves as a stock for the second, the second for the third. Thus we scale the ladder, step by step. And thence it happens that he who has mounted highest has often more honor than merit; for he has only mounted one speck higher on the shoulders of the next last.

^BHow often and perhaps how stupidly have I ex- 220 tended my book to make it speak of itself! ^CStupidly, if only for this reason, that I should have remembered what I say of others who do the same: that these frequent sheep's eyes at their own work testify that their heart thrills with love for it, and that even the rough, disdainful blows with which they beat it are only the love taps and affectations of maternal fondness; in keeping with Aristotle, to whom self-appreciation and self-depreciation often spring from the same sort of arrogance. For as for my excuse, that 230

I ought to have more liberty in this than others,
precisely because I write of myself and my writings
as of my other actions, because my theme turns in
upon itself—I do not know whether everyone will
accept it.

[B] I have observed in Germany that Luther has left
as many divisions and altercations over the uncertainty
of his opinions, and more, as he raised about the
Holy Scriptures.

240   Our disputes are purely verbal. I ask what is "nature," "pleasure," "circle," "substitution." The
question is one of words, and is answered in the same
way. "A stone is a body." But if you pressed on:
"And what is a body?"—"Substance."—"And what
is substance?" and so on, you would finally drive
the respondent to the end of his lexicon. We exchange
one word for another word, often more unknown.
I know better what is man than I know what is animal,
or mortal, or rational. To satisfy one doubt, they give
250 me three; it is the Hydra's head.

Socrates asked Meno what virtue was. "There is,"
said Meno, "the virtue of a man and of a woman,
of a magistrate and of a private individual, of a child
and of an old man." "That's fine," exclaimed Socrates; "we were in search of one virtue, and here
is a whole swarm of them."

We put one question, they give us back a hive of
them. As no event and no shape is entirely like another,
so none is entirely different from another. [C] An ingen-
260 ious mixture on the part of nature. If our faces were
not similar, we could not distinguish man from beast;
if they were not dissimilar, we could not distinguish
man from man. [B] All things hold together by some
similarity; every example is lame, and the comparison
that is drawn from experience is always faulty and
imperfect; however, we fasten together our compari-
sons by some corner. Thus the laws serve, and thus
adapt themselves to each of our affairs, by some
roundabout, forced, and biased interpretation.

270   Since the ethical laws, which concern the individual

duty of each man in himself, are so hard to frame, as we see they are, it is no wonder if those that govern so many individuals are more so....

[B]No judge has yet, thank God, spoken to me as a judge in any cause whatever, my own or another man's, criminal or civil. No prison has received me, not even for a visit. Imagination makes the sight of one, even from the outside, unpleasant to me. I am so sick for freedom, that if anyone should forbid me access to some corner of the Indies, I should live 280 distinctly less comfortably. And as long as I find earth or air open elsewhere, I shall not lurk in any place where I have to hide. Lord, how ill could I endure the condition in which I see so many people, nailed down to one section of this kingdom, deprived of the right to enter the principal towns and the courts and to use the public roads, for having quarreled with our laws! If those that I serve threatened even the tip of my finger, I should instantly go and find others, wherever it might be. All my little prudence in these 290 civil wars in which we are now involved is employed to keep them from interrupting my freedom of coming and going.

Now laws remain in credit not because they are just, but because they are laws. That is the mystic foundation of their authority; they have no other. [C]And that is a good thing for them. They are often made by fools, more often by people who, in their hatred of equality, are wanting in equity; but always by men, vain and irresolute authors.   300

There is nothing so grossly and widely and ordinarily faulty as the laws. [B]Whoever obeys them because they are just, does not obey them for just the reason he should. Our French laws, by their irregularity and lack of form, rather lend a hand to the disorder and corruption that is seen in their administration and execution. Their commands are so confused and inconsistent that they are some excuse for both dis-   ·
obedience and faulty interpretation, administration, and observance.   310

Then whatever may be the fruit we can reap from experience, what we derive from foreign examples will hardly be much use for our education, if we make such little profit from the experience we have of ourselves, which is more familiar to us, and certainly sufficient to inform us of what we need.

I study myself more than any other subject. That is my metaphysics, that is my physics.

> By what art God our home, the world, controls;
> 320 Whence the moon rises, where she sets, how rolls
> Her horns together monthly, and again
> Grows full; whence come the winds that rule the main;
> Where Eurus' blast holds sway; whence springs the rain
> That ever fills the clouds; [C]whether some day
> The citadels of the world will pass away.

PROPERTIUS

> [B]Inquire, you who the laboring world survey.

LUCAN

[C]In this universe of things I ignorantly and negli-
330 gently let myself be guided by the general law of the world. I shall know it well enough when I feel it. My knowledge could not make it change its path; it will not modify itself for me. It is folly to hope it, and greater folly to be troubled about it, since it is necessarily uniform, public, and common. The goodness and capacity of the governor should free us absolutely and fully from worrying about his government.

Philosophical inquiries and meditations serve only
340 as food for our curiosity. The philosophers with much reason refer us to the rules of Nature: but these have no concern with such sublime knowledge. The philosophers falsify them and show us the face of Nature painted in too high a color, and too sophisticated, whence spring so many varied portraits of so uniform a subject. As she has furnished us with feet to walk with, so she has given us wisdom to guide us in life: a wisdom not so ingenious, robust, and pompous as

that of their invention, but correspondingly easy and
salutary, performing very well what the other talks 350
about, in a man who has the good fortune to know
how to occupy himself simply and in an orderly way,
that is to say naturally. The more simply we trust
to Nature, the more wisely we trust to her. Oh, what
a sweet and soft and healthy pillow is ignorance and
incuriosity, to rest a well-made head!

^BI would rather be an authority on myself than
on ^CCicero.² ^BIn the experience I have of myself
I find enough to make me wise, if I were a good
scholar. He who calls back to mind the excess of 360
his past anger, and how far this fever carried him
away, sees the ugliness of this passion better than
in Aristotle, and conceives a more justified hatred
for it. He who remembers the evils he has undergone,
and those that have threatened him, and the slight
causes that have changed him from one state to
another, prepares himself in that way for future
changes and for recognizing his condition. The life
of Caesar has no more to show us than our own;
an emperor's or an ordinary man's, it is still a life 370
subject to all human accidents. Let us only listen:
we tell ourselves all we most need.

He who remembers having been mistaken so many,
many times in his own judgment, is he not a fool
if he does not distrust it forever after? When I find
myself convicted of a false opinion by another man's
reasoning, I do not so much learn what new thing
he has told me and this particular bit of ignorance—that
would be small gain—as I learn my weakness in
general, and the treachery of my understanding; 380
whence I derive the reformation of the whole mass.
With all my other errors I do the same, and I feel
that this rule is very useful for my life. I do not
regard the species and the individual, like a stone
I have stumbled on; I learn to mistrust my gait

2. The 1588 edition read: "than on Plato."

throughout, and I strive to regulate it. ^CTo learn that we have said or done a foolish thing, that is nothing; we must learn that we are nothing but fools, a far broader and more important lesson.

390   ^BThe slips that my memory has made so often, even when it reassures me most about itself, are not vainly lost on me; there is no use in her swearing to me now and assuring me, I shake my ears. The first opposition offered to her testimony puts me in suspense, and I would not dare trust her in any weighty matter, or guarantee her in another person's affairs. And were it not that what I do for lack of memory, others do still more often for lack of good faith, I should always accept the truth in matters of fact from
400 another man's mouth rather than from my own.

If each man watched closely the effects and circumstances of the passions that dominate him, as I have done with the ones I have fallen prey to, he would see them coming and would check their impetuosity and course a bit. They do not always leap at our throats at a single bound; there are threats and degrees.

> As when a rising wind makes white waves fly,
> The sea heaves slowly, raises billows high,
> And surges from the depths to meet the sky.

410   VIRGIL

Judgment holds in me a magisterial seat, at least it carefully tries to. It lets my feelings go their way, both hatred and friendship, even the friendship I bear myself, without being changed and corrupted by them. If it cannot reform the other parts according to itself, at least it does not let itself be deformed to match them; it plays its game apart.

The advice to everyone to know himself must have an important effect, since the god of learning and
420 light had it planted on the front of his temple, as comprising all the counsel he had to give us. ^CPlato also says that wisdom is nothing else but the execution of this command, and Socrates, in Xenophon, verifies it in detail.

^BThe difficulties and obscurity in any science are perceived only by those who have access to it. For a man needs at least some degree of intelligence to be able to notice that he does not know; and we must push against a door to know that it is closed to us. ^CWhence arises this Platonic subtlety, that 430 neither those who know need inquire, since they know, nor those who do not know, since in order to inquire they must know what they are inquiring about. ^BThus in this matter of knowing oneself, the fact that everyone is seen to be so cocksure and self-satisfied, that everyone thinks he understands enough about himself, signifies that everyone understands nothing about it, ^Cas Socrates teaches Euthydemus in Xenophon.

^BI, who make no other profession, find in me such infinite depth and variety, that what I have learned 440 bears no other fruit than to make me realize how much I still have to learn. To my weakness, so often recognized, I owe the inclination I have to modesty, obedience to the beliefs that are prescribed me, a constant coolness and moderation in my opinions, and my hatred for that aggressive and quarrelsome arrogance that believes and trusts wholly in itself, a mortal enemy of discipline and truth. Hear them laying down the law: the first stupidities that they advance are in the style in which men establish religions and laws. 450 ^C*Nothing is more discreditable than to have assertion and proof precede knowledge and perception* [Cicero].

^BAristarchus used to say that in former times there were scarcely seven wise men in the world, and that in his time there were scarcely seven ignorant men. Would we not have more reason than he to say that in our time? Affirmation and opinionativeness are express signs of stupidity. This man must have fallen on his nose a hundred times in one day; there he stands on his "ergos,"[3] as positive and unshaken as 460

3. Montaigne's word, *ergots*, means the spurs or hackles of a gamecock. But it also may mean *ergos* or *ergotisms*, the quibbling use of Latin *ergo* (therefore) by a choplogic (see Rabelais, *Pantagruel*, chap. 10).

before. You would think that someone had since
infused in him some sort of new soul and intellectual
vigor, and that he was like that ancient son of the
earth, who renewed his courage and strength by his
fall:

> Whose limbs, however tired,
> By touching Mother Earth, with energy were fired.

LUCAN

Does not this headstrong incorrigible think that he
470 picks up a new mind by picking up a new argument?

It is from my experience that I affirm human
ignorance, which is, in my opinion, the most certain
fact in the school of the world. Those who will not
conclude their own ignorance from so vain an example
as mine, or as theirs, let them recognize it through
Socrates, ᶜthe master of masters. For the philosopher
Antisthenes used to say to his pupils: "Let us go,
you and I, to hear Socrates; there I shall be a pupil
with you." And, maintaining this doctrine of his Stoic
480 sect, that virtue was enough to make a life fully happy
and free from need of anything whatever, he would
add: "Excepting the strength of Socrates."

ᴮThis long attention that I devote to studying myself
trains me also to judge passably of others, and there
are few things of which I speak more felicitously and
excusably. It often happens that I see and distinguish
the characters of my friends more exactly than they
do themselves. I have astonished at least one by the
pertinence of my description, and have given him
490 information about himself. ...

Experience has further taught me this, that we ruin
ourselves by impatience. Troubles have their life and
their limits, ᶜtheir illnesses and their health.

The constitution of diseases is patterned after the
constitution of animals. They have their destiny,
limited from their birth, and their days. He who tries
to cut them short imperiously by force, in the midst
of their course, prolongs and multiplies them, and
stimulates them instead of appeasing them. I agree

with Crantor, that we must neither obstinately and 500
heedlessly oppose evils nor weakly succumb to them,
but give way to them naturally, according to their
condition and our own. ᴮWe should give free passage
to diseases; and I find that they do not stay so long
with me, who let them go ahead; and some of those
that are considered most stubborn and tenacious, I
have shaken off by their own decadence, without help
and without art, and against the rules of medicine.
Let us give Nature a chance; she knows her business
better than we do. "But so-and-so died of it." So 510
will you, if not of that disease, of some other. And
how many have not failed to die of it, with three
doctors at their backsides? Example is a hazy mirror,
reflecting all things in all ways. If it is a pleasant
medicine, take it; it is always that much present gain.
ᶜI shall never balk at the name or the color, if it
is delicious and appetizing. Pleasure is one of the
principal kinds of profit.

ᴮI have allowed colds, gouty discharges, looseness,
palpitations of the heart, migraines, and other ailments 520
to grow old and die a natural death within me; I lost
them when I had half trained myself to harbor them.
They are conjured better by courtesy than by defiance.
We must meekly suffer the laws of our condition.
We are born to grow old, to grow weak, to be sick,
in spite of all medicine. That is the first lesson that
the Mexicans give their children, when, as soon as
they come out of their mother's womb, they greet
them thus: "Child, you have come into the world
to endure; endure, suffer, and keep quiet."   530

It is unjust to complain that what may happen to
anyone has happened to someone. ᶜ*Complain if anything has been unjustly decreed against you alone*
[Seneca]. ᴮLook at an old man praying God to keep
him in entire and vigorous health, that is to say, to
restore his youth.

Fool, why aspire in vain with childish prayers?
                                              OVID

Is it not madness? His condition does not allow it.
540 ^CThe gout, the stone, indigestion, are symptoms of
length of years, as are heat, rains, and winds of long
journeys. Plato does not believe that Aesculapius was
at any pains to attempt by treatment to prolong life
in a wasted and feeble body, useless to its country,
useless to its calling and for producing healthy, robust
children; and he does not consider such concern
consistent with divine justice and forethought, which
should guide all things toward utility. ^BMy good man,
it is all over. No one can put you on your feet again;
550 at most they will plaster and prop you up a bit, ^Cand
prolong your misery an hour or so:

> ^BLike one who, wishing to support a while
> A tottering building, props the creaking pile,
> Until one day the house, the props, and all
> Together with a dreadful havoc fall.

MAXIMIANUS

We must learn to endure what we cannot avoid.
Our life is composed, like the harmony of the world,
of contrary things, also of different tones, sweet and
560 harsh, sharp and flat, soft and loud. If a musician
liked only one kind, what would he have to say? He
must know how to use them together and blend them.
And so must we do with good and evil, which are
consubstantial with our life. Our existence is impossible without this mixture, and one element is no less
necessary for it than the other. To try to kick against
natural necessity is to imitate the folly of Ctesiphon,
who undertook a kicking match with his mule.

I do little consulting about the ailments I feel, for
570 these doctors are domineering when they have you
at their mercy. They scold at your ears with their
forebodings. And once, catching me weakened by
illness, they treated me insultingly with their dogmas
and magisterial frowns, threatening me now with great
pains, now with approaching death. I was not floored
by them or dislodged from my position, but I was
bumped and jostled. If my judgment was neither

changed nor confused by them, it was at least bothered. It is still agitation and struggle.

Now I treat my imagination as gently as I can, 580 and would relieve it, if I could, of all trouble and conflict. We must help it and flatter it, and fool it if we can. My mind is suited to this service; it has no lack of plausible reasons for all things. If it could persuade as well as it preaches, it would help me out very happily.

Would you like an example? It tells me that it is for my own good that I have the stone; that buildings of my age must naturally suffer some leakage. It is time for them to begin to grow loose and give way. 590 It is a common necessity—otherwise would it not have been a new miracle performed for me? Thereby I pay the tribute due to old age, and I could not get a better bargain.—That the company should console me, since I have fallen into the commonest ailment of men of my time of life. On all sides I see them afflicted with the same type of disease, and their society is honorable for me, since it preferably attacks the great; it is essentially noble and dignified.—That of the men who are stricken by it there are few that 600 get off more cheaply; and at that, they pay the penalty of an unpleasant diet and daily doses of loathsome medicinal drugs, whereas I am indebted solely to my good fortune. For a few ordinary broths of eryngo and rupturewort that I have swallowed two or three times to please the ladies, who, with kindness greater than the sharpness of my pain, offered me half of theirs, seemed to me as easy to take as they were useless in their effect. The others have to pay a thousand vows to Aesculapius, and as many crowns 610 to their doctor, for the easy and abundant outflow of gravel which I often get through the kindness of nature. ^C Even the propriety of my behavior in ordinary company is not disturbed by it, and I can hold my water ten hours and as long as anyone.

^B "Fear of this disease," says my mind, "used to terrify you, when it was unknown to you; the cries

and despair of those who make it worse by their lack
of fortitude engendered in you a horror of it. It is
620 an affliction that punishes those of your members
by which you have most sinned. You are a man of
conscience:

> Punishment undeserved gives pain.
>
> OVID

Consider this chastisement; it is very gentle in comparison with others, and paternally tender. Consider
its lateness; it bothers and occupies only the season
of your life which in any case is henceforth wasted
and barren, having given way, as if by agreement,
630 to the licentiousness and pleasures of your youth.

"The fear and pity that people feel for this illness
is a subject of vainglory for you; a quality of which,
even if you have purged your judgment and cured
your reason of it, your friends still recognize some
tincture in your makeup. There is pleasure in hearing
people say about you: There indeed is strength, there
indeed is fortitude! They see you sweat in agony,
turn pale, turn red, tremble, vomit your very blood,
suffer strange contractions and convulsions, some-
640 times shed great tears from your eyes, discharge thick,
black, and frightful urine, or have it stopped up by
some sharp rough stone that cruelly pricks and flays
the neck of your penis; meanwhile keeping up conversation with your company with a normal countenance,
jesting in the intervals with your servants, holding
up your end in a sustained discussion, making excuses
for your pain and minimizing your suffering.

"Do you remember those men of past times who
sought out troubles with such great hunger, to keep
650 their virtue in breath and in practice? Put the case
this way, that nature is bearing and pushing you into
that glorious school, which you would never have
entered of your own free will. If you tell me that
it is a dangerous and mortal disease, what others are
not? For it is a doctor's trick to except some, which
they say do not lead in a straight line to death. What

does it matter if they go there by accident and slip and deviate easily toward the road that leads us there?

C"But you do not die of being sick, you die of being alive. Death kills you well enough without the 660 help of illness. And illnesses have put off death for some, who have lived longer for thinking that they were on their way out and dying. Furthermore, there are diseases, as there are wounds, that are medicinal and salutary.

B"The stone is often no less fond of life than you. We see men in whom it has continued from their childhood up to their extreme old age; and if they had not deserted it, it was ready to accompany them still further. You kill it more often than it kills you; 670 and even if it set before you the picture of imminent death, would it not be a kind service for a man of that age to bring him home to meditations upon his end?

C"And what is worse, you have no reason left for being cured. In any case, the common fate will call you any day. B Consider how artfully and gently the stone weans you from life and detaches you from the world; not forcing you with tyrannical subjections, like so many other afflictions that you see in old people, 680 which keep them continually hobbled and without relief from infirmities and pains, but by warnings and instructions repeated at intervals, intermingled with long pauses for rest, as if to give you a chance to meditate and repeat its lesson at your leisure. To give you a chance to form a sound judgment and make up your mind to it like a brave man, it sets before you the lot that is your condition, the good and also the bad, and a life that on the same day is now very joyous, now unbearable. If you do not embrace death, 690 at least you shake hands with it once a month. C Whereby you have the further hope that it will catch you some day without a threat, and that, being so often led to the port, confident that you are still within the accustomed limits, some morning you and your confidence will have crossed the water unawares. B We

have no cause for complaint about illnesses that divide
the time fairly with health."

        I am obliged to Fortune for assailing me so often
700 with the same kind of weapons. She fashions and
trains me against them by use, hardens and accustoms
me. Henceforth I know just about at what cost I
shall be quit of them. ...

        [B] I, who operate only close to the ground, hate that
inhuman wisdom that would make us disdainful enemies of the cultivation of the body. I consider it equal
injustice to set our heart against natural pleasures
and to set our heart too much on them. [C] Xerxes was
a fool, who, wrapped in all human pleasures, went
710 and offered a prize to anyone who would find him
others. But hardly less of a fool is the man who cuts
off those that nature has found for him. [B] We should
neither pursue them nor flee them, we should accept
them. I accept them with more gusto and with better
grace than most, and more willingly let myself follow
a natural inclination. [C] We have no need to exaggerate
their inanity; it makes itself felt enough and evident
enough. Much thanks to our sickly, kill-joy mind,
which disgusts us with them as well as with itself.
720 It treats both itself and all that it takes in, whether
future or past, according to its insatiable, erratic, and
versatile nature.

        Unless the vessel's pure, all you pour in turns sour.

                                                    HORACE

        I, who boast of embracing the pleasures of life so
assiduously and so particularly, find in them, when
I look at them thus minutely, virtually nothing but
wind. But what of it? We are all wind. And even
the wind, more wisely than we, loves to make a noise
730 and move about, and is content with its own functions,
without wishing for stability and solidity, qualities that
do not belong to it.

        The pure pleasures of imagination, as well as the
pains, some say, are the greatest, as the scales of
Critolaus expressed it. No wonder; it composes them

to its liking and cuts them out of whole cloth. I see signal, and perhaps desirable, examples of this every day. But I, being of a mixed constitution, and coarse, am unable to cling so completely to this single and simple object as to keep myself from grossly pursuing 740 the present pleasures of the general human law—intellectually sensual, sensually intellectual. The Cyrenaic philosophers hold that the bodily pleasures, like the pains, are the more powerful, as being both twofold and more equitable.

^BThere are some who ^Cfrom savage stupidity, as Aristotle says, ^Bare disgusted with them; I know some who are that way from ambition. Why do they not also give up breathing? Why do they not live on their own air, ^Cand refuse light, because it is free and costs 750 them neither invention nor vigor? ^BLet Mars, or Pallas, or Mercury give them sustenance, instead of Venus, Ceres, and Bacchus, just to see what happens. ^CWon't they try to square the circle while perched on their wives! ^BI hate to have people order us to keep our minds in the clouds while our bodies are at table. I would not have the mind nailed down to it nor wallowing at it, but attending to it; ^Csitting at it, not lying down at it.

Aristippus defended the body alone, as if we had 760 no soul; Zeno embraced only the soul, as if we had no body. Both were wrong. Pythagoras, they say, followed a philosophy that was all contemplation, Socrates one that was all conduct and action; Plato found the balance between the two. But they say so to make a good story, and the true balance is found in Socrates, and Plato is much more Socratic than Pythagorean, and it becomes him better.

^BWhen I dance, I dance; when I sleep, I sleep; yes, and when I walk alone in a beautiful orchard, 770 if my thoughts have been dwelling on extraneous incidents for some part of the time, for some other part I bring them back to the walk, to the orchard, to the sweetness of this solitude, and to me. Nature has observed this principle like a mother, that the

actions she has enjoined on us for our need should also give us pleasure; and she invites us to them not only through reason, but also through appetite. It is unjust to infringe her laws.

780   When I see both Caesar and Alexander, in the thick of their great tasks, so fully enjoying ^Cnatural and therefore necessary and just ^Bpleasures, I do not say that that is relaxing their souls, I say that it is toughening them, subordinating these violent occupations and laborious thoughts, by the vigor of their spirits, to the practice of everyday life: ^Cwise men, had they believed that this was their ordinary occupation, the other the extraordinary.

We are great fools. "He has spent his life in
790   idleness," we say; "I have done nothing today." What, have you not lived? That is not only the fundamental but the most illustrious of your occupations. "If I had been placed in a position to manage great affairs, I would have shown what I could do." Have you been able to think out and manage your own life? You have done the greatest task of all. To show and exploit her resources Nature has no need of fortune; she shows herself equally on all levels and behind a curtain as well as without one. To compose our
800   character is our duty, not to compose books, and to win, not battles and provinces, but order and tranquillity in our conduct. Our great and glorious masterpiece is to live appropriately. All other things, ruling, hoarding, building, are only little appendages and props, at most.

^BI take pleasure in seeing an army general, at the foot of a breach that he means to attack presently, lending himself wholly and freely to his dinner and his conversation, among his friends; ^Cand Brutus, with
810   heaven and earth conspiring against him and Roman liberty, stealing some hour of night from his rounds to read and annotate Polybius with complete assurance. ^BIt is for little souls, buried under the weight of business, to be unable to detach themselves cleanly from it or to leave it and pick it up again:

> Brave men, who have endured with me
> Worse things, now banish cares with revelry;
> Tomorrow we shall sail the mighty sea.

HORACE

Whether it is in jest or in earnest that the Sorbonne 820
acquired its proverbial reputation for theological
drinking and feasting, I think it right that the faculty
should dine all the more comfortably and pleasantly
for having used the morning profitably and seriously
in the work of their school. The consciousness of
having spent the other hours well is a proper and
savory sauce for the dinner table. Thus did the sages
live. And that inimitable straining for virtue that
astounds us in both Catos, that disposition, severe
to the point of being troublesome, submitted thus 830
meekly and contentedly to the laws of human nature,
and of Venus and Bacchus, ^Cin accordance with the
precepts of their sect, which require the perfect sage
to be as expert and versed in the enjoyment of the
natural pleasures as in any other duty of life. *A wise
palate should go with a wise heart* [Cicero].

^BRelaxation and affability, it seems to me, are
marvelously honorable and most becoming to a strong
and generous soul. Epaminondas did not think that
to mingle with the dance of the boys of his city, 840
^Cto sing, to play music, ^Band to concentrate attentively
on these things, was at all derogatory to the honor
of his glorious victories and the perfect purity of
character that was his. And among so many admirable
actions of Scipio, ^Cthe grandfather, a personage
worthy of the reputation of celestial descent,[4] ^Bthere
is nothing that lends him more charm than to see
him playing nonchalantly and childishly at picking up
and selecting shells and running potato races by the
sea with Laelius, and in bad weather amusing and 850
tickling his fancy by writing comedies portraying the

4. Instead of this phrase, Montaigne had written in 1588: "Scipio
the Younger (everything considered, the first man of the Romans)."
His first attribution was the correct one.

meanest and most vulgar actions of men; ^Cand, his head full of that wonderful campaign against Hannibal and Africa, visiting the schools in Sicily, and attending lectures on philosophy until he armed to the teeth the blind envy of his enemies in Rome. ^BNor is there anything more remarkable in Socrates than the fact that in his old age he finds time to take lessons in dancing and playing instruments, and considers it well

860 spent.

This same man was once seen standing in a trance, an entire day and night, in the presence of the whole Greek army, overtaken and enraptured by some deep thought. He was seen, ^Cthe first among so many valiant men of the army, to run to the aid of Alcibiades, who was overwhelmed by enemies, to cover him with his body, and to extricate him from the melee by sheer force of arms; and the first among the people of Athens, all outraged like him at such a shameful

870 spectacle, to come forward to rescue Theramenes, whom the Thirty Tyrants were having led to his death by their satellites; and he desisted from this bold undertaking only at the remonstrance of Theramenes himself, though he was followed by only two men in all. He was seen, when courted by a beauty with whom he was in love, to maintain strict chastity when necessary. He was seen, in the battle of Delium, to pick up and save Xenophon, who had been thrown from his horse. He was ^Bconstantly ^Cseen ^Bto march

880 to war ^Cand walk the ice ^Bbarefoot, to wear the same gown in winter and in summer, to surpass all his companions in enduring toil, to eat no differently at a feast than ordinarily.

^CHe was seen for twenty-seven years to endure with the same countenance hunger, poverty, the indocility of his children, the claws of his wife; and in the end calumny, tyranny, prison, irons, and poison. ^BBut if that man was summoned to a drinking bout by the duty of civility, he was also the one who did

890 the best in the whole army. And he never refused to play at cobnut with children, or to ride a hobbyhorse

with them, and he did so gracefully; for all actions, says philosophy, are equally becoming and honorable in a wise man. We have material enough, and we should never tire of presenting the picture of this man as a pattern and ideal of all sorts of perfection. ^CThere are very few full and pure examples of life, and those who educate us are unfair when they set before us every day feeble and defective models, hardly good in a single vein, which rather pull us 900 backward, corrupters rather than correctors.

^BPopular opinion is wrong: it is much easier to go along the sides, where the outer edge serves as a limit and a guide, than by the middle way, wide and open, and to go by art than by nature; but it is also much less noble and less commendable. ^CGreatness of soul is not so much pressing upward and forward as knowing how to set oneself in order and circumscribe oneself. It regards as great whatever is adequate, and shows its elevation by liking moderate things better 910 than eminent ones. ^BThere is nothing so beautiful and legitimate as to play the man well and properly, no knowledge so hard to acquire as the knowledge of how to live this life well ^Cand naturally; ^Band the most barbarous of our maladies is to despise our being.

He who wants to detach his soul, let him do it boldly, if he can, when his body is ill, to free it from the contagion; at other times, on the contrary, let the soul assist and favor the body and not refuse to take part in its natural pleasures and enjoy them 920 conjugally, bringing to them moderation, if it is the wiser of the two, for fear that through lack of discretion they may merge into pain. ^CIntemperance is the plague of sensual pleasure; and temperance is not its scourge, it is its seasoning. Eudoxus, who made pleasure the supreme good, and his fellows, who raised it to such high value, savored it in its most charming sweetness by means of temperance, which they possessed in singular and exemplary degree.

^BI order my soul to look upon both pain and pleasure 930 with a gaze equally ^Cself-controlled—*for it is as wrong*

*for the soul to overflow from joy as to contract in
sorrow* [Cicero]—and equally ^Bfirm, but gaily at the
one, at the other severely, and, according to its ability,
as anxious to extinguish the one as to extend the
other. ^CViewing good things sanely implies viewing
bad things sanely. And pain has something not to
be avoided in its mild beginning, and pleasure something to be avoided in its excessive ending. Plato
940 couples them together and claims that it is equally
the function of fortitude to fight against pain and
against the immoderate and bewitching blandishments
of pleasure. They are two fountains: whoever draws
the right amount from the right one at the right time,
whether city, man, or beast, is very fortunate. The
first we must take as a necessary medicine, but more
sparingly; the other for thirst, but not to the point
of drunkenness. Pain, pleasure, love, hatred, are the
first things a child feels; if when reason comes they
950 cling to her, that is virtue.

^BI have a vocabulary all my own. I "pass the time,"
when it is rainy and disagreeable; when it is good,
I do not want to pass it; I savor it, I cling to it.
We must run through the bad and settle on the good.
This ordinary expression "pastime" or "pass the
time" represents the habit of those wise folk who
think they can make no better use of their life than
to let it slip by and escape it, pass it by, sidestep
it, and, as far as in them lies, ignore it and run away
960 from it, as something irksome and contemptible. But
I know it to be otherwise and find it both agreeable
and worth prizing, even in its last decline, in which
I now possess it; and nature has placed it in our hands
adorned with such favorable conditions that we have
only ourselves to blame if it weighs on us and if
it escapes us unprofitably. ^C*The life of a fool is joyless,
full of trepidation, given over wholly to the future*
[Seneca]. ^BHowever, I am reconciling myself to the
thought of losing it, without regret, but as something
970 that by its nature must be lost; not as something
annoying and troublesome. ^CThen too, not to dislike

dying is properly becoming only to those who like
living. [B]It takes management to enjoy life. I enjoy
it twice as much as others, for the measure of enjoyment depends on the greater or lesser attention that
we lend it. Especially at this moment, when I perceive
that mine is so brief in time, I try to increase it in
weight; I try to arrest the speed of its flight by the
speed with which I grasp it, and to compensate for
the haste of its ebb by my vigor in using it. The   980
shorter my possession of life, the deeper and fuller
I must make it.

Others feel the sweetness of some satisfaction and
of prosperity; I feel it as they do, but it is not in
passing and slipping by. Instead we must study it,
savor it, and ruminate it, to give proper thanks for
it to him who grants it to us. They enjoy the other
pleasures as they do that of sleep, without being
conscious of them. To the end that sleep itself should
not escape me thus stupidly, at one time I saw fit   990
to have mine disturbed, so that I might gain a glimpse
of it. I meditate on any satisfaction; I do not skim
over it, I sound it, and bend my reason, now grown
peevish and hard to please, to welcome it. Do I find
myself in some tranquil state? Is there some voluptuous
pleasure that tickles me? I do not let my senses pilfer
it, I bring my soul into it, not to implicate herself,
but to enjoy herself, not to lose herself but to find
herself. And I set her, for her part, to admire herself
in this prosperous estate, to weigh and appreciate and 1000
amplify the happiness of it. She measures the extent
of her debt to God for being at peace with her
conscience and free from other inner passions, for
having her body in its natural condition, enjoying
controlledly and adequately the agreeable and pleasant
functions with which he is pleased to compensate by
his grace for the pains with which his justice chastises
us in its turn; how much it is worth to her to be
lodged at such a point that wherever she casts her
eyes, the sky is calm around her: no desire, no fear 1010
or doubt to disturb the air for her, no difficulty, [C]past,

present, or future, ^Bover which her imagination may not pass without hurt.

This consideration gains great luster by comparison between my condition and that of others. Thus I set before me in a thousand forms those who are carried away and tossed about by fortune or their own error, and also those, closer to my way, who accept their good fortune so languidly and indifferently. They are
1020 the people who really "pass their time"; they pass over the present and what they possess, to be the slaves of hope, and for shadows and vain images that fancy dangles before them—

> Like ghosts that after death are said to flit,
> Or visions that delude the slumbering wit
>
> VIRGIL

—which hasten and prolong their flight the more they are pursued. The fruit and goal of their pursuit is to pursue, as Alexander said that the purpose of his
1030 work was to work,

> Believing nothing done while aught was left to do.
>
> LUCAN

As for me, then, I love life and cultivate it just as God has been pleased to grant it to us. I do not go about wishing that it should lack the need to eat and drink, ^Cand it would seem to me no less excusable a failing to wish that need to be doubled. *The wise man is the keenest searcher for natural treasures* [Seneca]. Nor do I wish ^Bthat we should sustain
1040 ourselves by merely putting into our mouths a little of that drug by which Epimenides took away his appetite and kept himself alive; nor that we should beget children insensibly with our fingers or our heels, ^Cbut rather, with due respect, that we could also beget them voluptuously with our fingers and heels; nor ^Bthat the body should be without desire and without titillation. Those are ungrateful ^Cand unfair ^Bcomplaints. I accept with all my heart ^Cand with gratitude ^Bwhat nature has done for me, and I am pleased with

myself and proud of myself that I do. We wrong 1050
that great and all-powerful Giver by refusing his gift,
nullifying it, and disfiguring it. ^CHimself all good,
he has made all things good. *All things that are
according to nature are worthy of esteem* [Cicero].

^BOf the opinions of philosophy I most gladly em-
brace those that are most solid, that is to say, most
human and most our own; my opinions, in conformity
with my conduct, are low and humble. ^CPhilosophy
is very childish, to my mind, when she gets up on
her hind legs and preaches to us that it is a barbarous 1060
alliance to marry the divine with the earthly, the
reasonable with the unreasonable, the severe with the
indulgent, the honorable with the dishonorable; that
sensual pleasure is a brutish thing unworthy of being
enjoyed by the wise man; that the only pleasure he
derives from the enjoyment of a beautiful young wife
is the pleasure of his consciousness of doing the right
thing, like putting on his boots for a useful ride. May
her followers have no more right and sinews and sap
in deflowering their wives than her lessons have!   1070

That is not what Socrates says, her tutor and ours.
He prizes bodily pleasure as he should, but he prefers
that of the mind, as having more power, constancy,
ease, variety, and dignity. The latter by no means
goes alone, according to him—he is not so fanciful—
but only comes first. For him temperance is the
moderator, not the adversary, of pleasures.

^BNature is a gentle guide, but no more gentle than
wise and just. ^C*We must penetrate into the nature
of things and clearly see exactly what it demands* 1080
[Cicero]. ^BI seek her footprints everywhere. We have
confused them with artificial tracks, ^Cand for that
reason the sovereign good of the Academics and the
Peripatetics, which is "to live according to nature,"
becomes hard to limit and express; also that of the
Stoics, a neighbor to the other, which is "to consent
to nature."

^BIs it not an error to consider some actions less
worthy because they are necessary? No, they will

1090 not knock it out of my head that the marriage of
     pleasure with necessity, ^Cwith whom, says an ancient,
     the gods always conspire, ^Bis a very suitable one.
     To what purpose do we dismember by divorce a
     structure made up of such close and brotherly corre-
     spondence? On the contrary, let us bind it together
     again by mutual services. Let the mind arouse and
     quicken the heaviness of the body, and the body check
     and make fast the lightness of the mind. ^C*He who
     praises the nature of the soul as the sovereign good*
1100 *and condemns the nature of the flesh as evil, truly
     both carnally desires the soul and carnally shuns the
     flesh; for his feeling is inspired by human vanity, not
     by divine truth* [Saint Augustine].
          ^BThere is no part unworthy of our care in this gift
     that God has given us; we are accountable for it even
     to a single hair. And it is not a perfunctory charge
     to man to guide man according to his nature; it is
     express, simple, ^Cand of prime importance, ^Band the
     creator has given it to us seriously and sternly.
1110 ^CAuthority alone has power over common intelli-
     gences, and has more weight in a foreign language.
     Let us renew the charge here. *Who would not say
     that it is the essence of folly to do lazily and rebelliously
     what has to be done, to impel the body one way and
     the soul another, to be split between the most conflicting
     motions?* [Seneca.]
          ^BCome on now, just to see, some day get some
     man to tell you the absorbing thoughts and fancies
     that he takes into his head, and for the sake of which
1120 he turns his mind from a good meal and laments the
     time he spends on feeding himself. You will find there
     is nothing so insipid in all the dishes on your table
     as this fine entertainment of his mind (most of the
     time we should do better to go to sleep completely
     than to stay awake for what we do stay awake for);
     and you will find that his ideas and aspirations are
     not worth your stew. Even if they were the transports
     of Archimedes himself, what of it? I am not here

touching on, or mixing up with that brattish rabble of men that we are, or with the vanity of the desires 1130 and musings that distract us, those venerable souls, exalted by ardent piety and religion to constant and conscientious meditation on divine things, ^Cwho, anticipating, by dint of keen and vehement hope, the enjoyment of eternal food, final goal and ultimate limit of Christian desires, sole constant and incorruptible pleasure, scorn to give their attention to our beggardly, watery, and ambiguous comforts, and readily resign to the body the concern and enjoyment of sensual and temporal fodder. ^BThat is a privileged 1140 study. ^CBetween ourselves, these are two things that I have always observed to be in singular accord: supercelestial thoughts and subterranean conduct.

^BAesop, ^Cthat great man, ^Bsaw his master pissing as he walked. "What next?" he said. "Shall we have to shit as we run?" Let us manage our time; we shall still have a lot left idle and ill spent. Our mind likes to think it has not enough leisure hours to do its own business unless it dissociates itself from the body for the little time that the body really needs it.   1150

They want to get out of themselves and escape from the man. That is madness: instead of changing into angels, they change into beasts; instead of raising themselves, they lower themselves. ^CThese transcendental humors frighten me, like lofty and inaccessible places; and nothing is so hard for me to stomach in the life of Socrates as his ecstasies and possessions by his daemon, nothing is so human in Plato as the qualities for which they say he is called divine. ^BAnd of our sciences, those seem to me most terrestrial 1160 and low which have risen the highest. And I find nothing so humble and so mortal in the life of Alexander as his fancies about his immortalization. Philotas stung him wittily by his answer. He congratulated him by letter on the oracle of Jupiter Ammon which had lodged him among the gods: "As far as you are concerned, I am very glad of it; but there is reason to pity the men who will have to live with and obey a man who exceeds ^Cand is not content with ^Ba man's proportions."

> ^CSince you obey the gods, you rule the world.
>
> HORACE

^BThe nice inscription with which the Athenians honored the entry of Pompey into their city is in accord with my meaning.

> You are as much a god as you will own
> That you are nothing but a man alone.
>
> AMYOT'S PLUTARCH

It is an absolute perfection and virtually divine to know how to enjoy our being rightfully. We seek other conditions because we do not understand the use of our own, and go outside of ourselves because we do not know what it is like inside. ^CYet there is no use our mounting on stilts, for on stilts we must still walk on our own legs. And on the loftiest throne in the world we are still sitting only on our own rump.

^BThe most beautiful lives, to my mind, are those that conform to the common ^Chuman ^Bpattern, ^Cwith order, but ^Bwithout miracle and without eccentricity. Now old age needs to be treated a little more tenderly. Let us commend it to that god who is the protector of health and wisdom, but gay and sociable wisdom:

> Grant me but health, Latona's son,
> And to enjoy the wealth I've won,
> And honored age, with mind entire
> And not unsolaced by the lyre.
>
> HORACE